MW01230180

A KISS FROM A KRAKEN

KISS FROM A MONSTER SERIES BOOK 2

CHARLOTTE SWAN

This is a work of fiction. Names, characters, places, and incidents either are the product of the author's imagination or are used fictitiously. Any resemblance to actual persons, living or dead, events, or locales is entirely coincidental.

Copyright © 2023 by Charlotte Swan

All rights reserved. No part of this book may be reproduced or used in any manner without written permission of the copyright owner except for the use of quotations in a book review. For more information, address: authorcharlotteswan@gmail.com.

eBook ISBN: 979-8-9870192-5-2

Cover Design by Charlotte Swan

www.authorcharlotteswan.com

Created with Vellum

There's tentacles in here. So many tentacles...

CONTENT & TROPE INFORMATION

For more information regarding content warnings and tropes included in this novella please click here.

1

MELODY

This party was not my idea.

Well, none of them are, however, this one I was particularly against. My father didn't listen, something he's all too comfortable with doing these days. Once upon a time, my father would've rather cut off his right hand than see me sad. Would've tried tirelessly to coax a smile from me and we would've laughed together over this disgusting display of opulence in front of us tonight.

Four years ago, the dress I'm wearing right now would've fed us for months.

Four years ago, my father was a humble fisherman, one that was unluckier than most. He would come back every night with a few measly fish and a few gold coins to keep a rickety roof over our heads. After my mother passed he did everything to preserve her memory and to try and raise me to be a smart, strong young woman just like her.

To speak my mind, to never ever doubt my worth.

Then one night everything changed. I still remember it like it was yesterday. The barrels of fish he came in with that night. Fresh catches of lobsters, mussels, and even some shellfish that we hadn't seen in decades. All of which would fetch a high price with the nobility who ruled over our town.

Precious pearls were cleaved from the hard shells of oysters and sold at the market.

Overnight we became millionaires. By the end of the week, I had been ushered into this grand house on the Lord's Row, given a lady's maid and a governess to teach me how to function within our new wealth and standing. By the end of the month, my father was different. The wealth had turned him into a greedy, egotistical man and I realized the life I had known, the one my mother had wanted for me, was gone.

Just like her precious bag of pearls.

My father said they were lost in the move, but he couldn't meet my eyes when he told me. Whether it be from shame or something else I don't know. The only thing for certain is that those were her most prized possessions, one of the last things I have of her.

A loud crack of thunder breaks me from my thoughts. I tilt my head to the side and stare out of our massive window. The rain is coming down in sheets, and people below scurry to try and save their hair and clothes but it is useless. This storm is foreboding, the sky an inky black, illuminated by the swift strikes of lightning.

No one at this party seems to take notice.

Turning back to the room before me I suppress the urge to groan. Instead, I force my face into a cold mask of indifference. This is my father's third annual Fisherman's Ball, the title a mockery of our former lives as no one here has ever cast a net, let alone felt the salty spray of ocean water sting their sunburned skin after spending hours at sea. This is just another excuse for my father to revel in his greed and arrogance.

Our ballroom is adorned in all types of gaudy fashioning. Eight solid gold candelabras decorate the long, wood dining table I am sitting at. Dinner ended over an hour ago but I cannot bear to mingle with these people. I take a sip of wine and survey the scene before me.

I watch from behind one of our ridiculous place settings, a bouquet of white roses dotted with real pearls and seashells, as our attendees float around the room. Perfumed lords and ladies dance in their finery. Dresses that look like pastries swish along our marble floors; men dressed in overcoats that are cinched so tight it's a wonder they can breathe. Everyone is primped and polished and using this as a chance to flaunt their own wealth.

Reaching for my glass I catch myself in the mirror hanging across the ballroom. I barely recognize myself anymore. Physically I look the same. My red hair is curled, and the front pieces are pulled back from my face to highlight the pearl earrings I am wearing. Those same pearls are stitched into my light blue gown, matching the color of my eyes and making my fair complexion glow.

However, this creature staring back at me isn't the child who enjoyed the mud and swimming at low tide off our old dock. Who stayed up late while their mother told them legends of the monsters who lived in the sea. Who saw each day as a gift, a wondrous opportunity to explore new things.

Our new wealth has sucked that from me. Turned me into this manicured, docile version of myself that is meant to sit still and smile during meaningless pleasantries. This is not who I am, this is not who my father is.

Does this show of wealth not disgust him? Does he no longer remember who we used to be?

I cannot keep living like this. I have become his doll. A prop he introduces to men, in the hopes that my marriage to them will secure him more connections. He made that evident last year after I turned eighteen. I was a woman and my job is to become a wife and mother, my dreams, if I had any, were all to be forgotten.

Reaching for my wine glass, I look away from the mirror only to lock eyes with the one person I have been trying to avoid most this evening. Prince Edwind is the most repulsive man I have ever met. When he kissed my cheek at the beginning of the evening my nerve endings screamed. I had to hold myself back from rushing to the nearest washroom and scrubbing my skin raw to rid myself of his contact.

He is a few years older than me but already shows signs of decaying. An opulent life has allowed him to indulge in all things and his health suffers greatly for it. If Edwind makes it to fifty years of age the gods have been more than merciful.

"Lady Melody, will you do me the privilege of letting me lead you in this next dance?"

His breath smells of sweet wine and roasted meat. From my chair, I have to look up to meet his unfocused stare. Those bloodshot brown eyes wander down my chest, where the swells of my breasts have been pushed up due to the tight lacing of my gown. The Prince does not even try to hide his leer, licking his stained yellow teeth. Repulsive.

His gold cloak is starched, stitched with an even finer gold thread. His whole outfit sparkles in the candlelight. Greasy brown hair has been swept back from his reddish face. Rings dot every finger as he holds his sweaty palm out to me.

The question is a formality, the Prince would never think to be denied. Especially not by the likes of me.

Perhaps I have partaken in too much wine, perhaps this time sitting with myself, watching this all unfold has afforded me some clarity. I look past the Prince and see my father's eyes watching us. He nods slowly and silently orders me to accept the Prince's dance request.

Last year I would've done it; this year I refuse to take part in this any longer.

My father must still have some love for me. His only child. He is not so far lost to me that he would make me entertain this disgusting creature, prince or not. I have to believe somewhere deep down he is still that poor fisherman my mother loved. That poor fisherman, who loved our family more than anything.

That thought strengthens me and I straighten my spine.

"Unfortunately, Your Majesty, I have no desire to dance with anyone tonight. I am sure another young lady would be a more willing partner for you." I cut a glance over to the ten young women watching our exchange with rapt expressions. Shock widens the Prince's eyes as if this outcome was completely unexpected.

This should be interesting, I think as I take my final sip of wine.

"I don't understand."

"What is it you don't understand?" I ask. "I thought I spoke quite plainly."

"You are rejecting...my invitation to dance?"

"Yes."

"You cannot do that."

"And yet I have." Rising from the table, I snatch up my glass, intent on getting a refill of wine and effectively ending this conversation. Thick fingers grip my upper arm and I let out a gasp.

"No one rejects me, you cold wench," he sneers at me.

"Who do you think you are? I am your *Prince*, you and your family are nothing. You found fortune but that doesn't change the fact that you will always be beneath me."

"Get your hand off of—"

"Perhaps beneath me is where you are destined to stay." His grin is pure lecherous evil as he licks over his lips. My stomach rolls as I try again to yank my arm from his grasp. Prince Edwind tightens his grip on me and instinct takes over. My leg kicks out, directly into his most private, albeit *underwhelming*, parts.

The Prince crumples to the floor, crying in agony and clutching at his groin.

"Never," I spit out, "*never* touch me again."

"How dare you, traitorous bitch! I'll have your head for this!"

Death would be better than marrying that beast.

Loud footsteps sound as my father approaches. Our matching eyes connect, his are akin to blue flames as he takes in the scene. Tension tightens his muscles and I think for a second my old father is back. Anger on my behalf and he will surely kick this prince from our home for daring to touch me. He will comfort me and tell me he is sorry he did not protect me better.

"Melody!" my father yells. From his tone alone I can tell that my hopes of my old father's return are dashed. "Explain yourself, why have you hurt the Prince in this way? He sought me out this evening in the hopes of me approving your courtship, which I did! You ungrateful child, you have hurt your potential husband."

"He grabbed me, Father, made it seem like he would—"

"It does not matter." My father is quick to cut me off. "You need to do your duty, child. You have dishonored me tonight. What man of standing will take you now?"

Shock puts ice in my veins. *He does not care what the Prince planned on doing to me. That whatever he wanted I need to go along with so long as he gave his word to my father that he would marry me.* With that sinking realization I understand now just how stupid I had been.

My father is lost. I lost him that day he came home with all the fish and the jewels. The man I once knew, the man I had loved, my true father died that morning.

I open my mouth to finally unleash all the things I've been holding back from saying when another crack of thunder sounds. This time it seems to come from right over the house, shaking the walls so hard portraits crash to the floor. On the second boom, my glass slides from my hand, shattering at my feet. Everyone is crying out trying to determine what could be the cause of this when our front door bursts open.

The heavy oak door slams against the wall and we watch in horror as salty, seawater begins to free-flow into our house. It is impossible, we are several hundred feet above sea level. If we are flooding, the people below us have no hope of surviving this storm.

A few cries of outrage can be heard as people start scrambling up on tables. My delicate shoes are soaked through, and the icy water stops just below my knees, making my dress feel extra heavy.

Immediately I start to shiver, the temperature plummeting until I can see my breath curling in front of me.

A few partygoers begin to shout that we should call for help when it happens. Another flash of lightning illuminates the scene before us. Massive blue, meaty tentacles come slipping through the front door. Slithering through the cold water in soft ripples. Stretching over the door frame, taking up the whole entryway until it pushes through, its enormous suckers sticking onto the sides for leverage.

The tentacles twist over each other, like a massive ball of suckers and muscles rolling towards us through the water. A pair of blazing red eyes peers out from inside of them. Completely red, with no pupils or whites. They survey the room, landing on me for a moment. A shiver runs down my spine but I note with some mild horror that it is not fear making my stomach tighten. Before I can examine that emotion too deeply, its eyes drift from me and lock in on my father.

This creature can only be one thing. A mythical creature, used as a cautionary tale to scare children into behaving and sailors to be wary on the high seas. However, there is no denying what is in front of us now. And if it is here...

"Percy Rivers." The voice sounds straight out of a nightmare. As deep and resounding as a fog horn. My eyes shoot over to my father whose fair skin has turned even paler.

"That's him!" Someone shouts from the crowd and my father's knees wobble as he takes a step forward toward the creature. Breathing rapidly, each of his exhales are white puffs that form in sync with the beat of my heart. Turning towards the creature, I try my best to keep my spine straight as I take in the sight before me.

One thing is clear: my father must have done something terrible for this creature to be seeking him out.

"Do you know who I am?" The voice booms again, scraping over my skin and freezing the blood in my veins. The sound is so ancient and evil, so raw and...powerful. My own knees threaten to buckle under the weight of it.

"Y—yes—s," stutters my father.

"Say it," the creature commands.

"You—you're the Kraken of the Darksea. God of the Tides and of the Ocean."

A few gasps go up in the room. Despite their distance from the actual work of fishermen, this is a seaside town. All children, regardless of wealth and title, are taught the stories of the Kraken. To not swim in dark water or it will drag you down to live in its cursed kingdom, feasting on your bones for eternity.

Within each myth is a bit of truth and it seems the legend of the Kraken of the Darksea hadn't been exaggerated at all.

"A god, he calls me," snickers the Kraken, "yet you so recklessly steal from me. Thinking you will avoid all punishment for doing so."

A small sound leaves me as I turn towards my father. He is a lot of things, especially as of late, but a thief? I guess he is an idiot as well because who in this world would think to rob the Kraken of all beings?

"I don't know what you are—"

"Do not deny it," the Kraken cuts him off. "Lying will not help your case, nothing will. I know every step you have taken since I first became aware of your treachery, Percy Rivers. The sea rewards those who deserve to be rewarded. You took more from it, from me, than you were owed through a trick. A bargain with that fiend in *The Woods*. A demon you sought out in a moment of greed." He pauses, his tentacles slipping and sliding around him through the dark water. "Bargained away a bag of pearls, if I'm not mistaken."

My world stops.

"No!" I shout. My father's muscles tense even further. "How could you? They were hers, *hers* and you gave them away without a second thought?"

My mind is racing. Does his treachery know no end? That was the price he paid for all of this? My outburst has caused the Kraken's eyes to turn on me, appraising me under those fiery orbs. I meet his stare, unafraid. My world has already been changed forever, what is a stare-down with a Kraken?

I want to launch myself at my father. To scream and kick and punch him, to hurt him, to make him understand the rage I have carried with me all these years. However, the Kraken of the Darksea moves faster. His eyes refocus on my father and his tentacles reach out, slipping along the marble floor beneath the shallow pool of water. They seem to grow larger as they expand until they finally wrap around the base of my father's legs.

"You will pay for your theft with your life."

My father screams, a blood-curdling sound that hurts my ears.

"Please, please," he begs, "please, Kraken of the Darksea, spare me. I only did it to save her." My father throws his arm out towards me, finally acknowledging my presence. How dare he claim this was all for me. "We were starving, I did it to keep her fed, to keep her clothed and safe."

Doesn't he understand I would've rather died than have lost that last piece of my mother? Instead, he parted with it in order to gain his change in luck, this new fortune, this house...all of it gotten by a bargain with the demon of *The Woods*.

The Kraken's red eyes land on me once more, appraising me from head to toe. A predator assessing its prey. Perhaps it finds me as culpable as my father and I shall be killed here too.

That thought makes me shake where I stand.

The dark water in front of me ripples and slowly, almost

cautiously, a slimmer tentacle reaches out toward me. It skims up the side of my body before brushing along my cheek. The tentacle tucks some of my hair behind my ear, playing with my dangling pearl earring, before gently suctioning onto my earlobe. I try not to weaken under his attention. If he means to kill me, I will face my death bravely.

Though a deep, dark part of me does not wish to recoil from his touch. There is something obscenely soothing about it. His tentacle is warm, his touch gentle and firm. The events of this night have clearly rendered me in shock.

That can be the only explanation.

"She is sweet," the Kraken rumbles, the sound tightening my nipples in my gown. What is happening to me?

"I'll offer this deal only once, fisherman." His tentacle leaves my cheek, falling gently into the water at my feet. "Since you stole something of mine, I will take something of yours. I will spare your life if you give your daughter to me instead."

A shocked sound falls from my lips.

Please, don't let him take me, I am your daughter. I will him to hear my plea, but it seems like my fate is already sealed. As I watch a spark of remorse cloud his blue eyes before they harden and I know his decision has been made.

He mouths *I'm sorry* before turning back to the Kraken of the Darksea.

"I agree to your deal, Kraken." The tentacle at my feet moves quickly, looping and tightening around my legs in a vice grip.

"No!" I scream. "You can't do this! You can't! Father, *father* please, you can't let him take me." My father is silent as I hear the splashes coming from more tentacles entering the water. "Somebody! Any of you, help me please!" No one moves a muscle. I watch in horror as more begin to loop around me, covering my legs completely. The creature only laughs, while my father remains silent.

"Fuck you!" I scream at my father. "Fuck all of you for not doing anything! For not helping me!"

I turn back to the creature as more water laps up against my legs. His massive form twists and rolls toward me, a mass of suckers and blue muscles. From inside the chaos, I hear the stomps of thick leather boots. My knees buckle as long, strong human legs are revealed clad in thick leather breeches, take confident steps toward me.

Refusing to look weak in the face of the Kraken, I try and hold my body still and lock eyes with his red gaze. He stands in front of me, so tall that I have to crane my neck back to keep eye contact with him. The tentacles wrapped around me have dissipated. All of them have retreated back towards where his head would be. Shorter, stopping just under his shoulders like he has a beard.

A beard of blue tentacles that move and snap on their own accord.

Those red eyes bore into mine. A stray tentacle coasts over my forehead as a blue, damp hand cups my chin. The warning is clear, his power is absolute. This is who my father gave me to. This is who holds my future in his hands.

"You're mine, sweet one." He gently pulls my chin down and a slippery tentacle takes a shallow thrust into my mouth. I cannot scream, I cannot move all I can do is stand there. One sucker attaches to my tongue and that is the last thing I remember before my shaking knees finally give out, and I plunge into the waiting darkness.

2

ZALENYK

Of all the wonders I have seen over the years, this human in my arms is the most precious.

Her pathetic thief of a father never desired this jewel. She is a treasure, one I will safeguard for the rest of eternity. I will protect her, shield her and she will belong to me. Everything I had before today means as much as old fish bones.

She is all there is for me now.

My tentacles tangle in her long, red hair. Such a wonderful color, something that you don't find in the sea. I can feel her softness everywhere with her wrapped in my limbs like this. The soft press of her breasts and the supple curve of her ass warm my skin as I hold her. When she fainted in my presence, I wasted no time scooping her up and getting into the long boat. One of my servants, a drowned pirate with an exposed jawbone and one missing eye, steers us carefully to my palace.

A watery death puts your soul into my eternal servitude.

My human shivers against me and I tighten my hold on her. She is so small I will have to remind myself to be gentle when the time comes. Already my body is screaming, clutching so much of her delicate softness has my cock hard. How easy would it be to rip her from her soaked gown, to fit my tentacles into the snug hole between her legs, her mouth...her ass.

I must be patient, for as much as I would like to do those things, I need to wait for her to be willing. I will not behave like my kind used to. Just like my father when he found his human bride, the thought of my treasure in pain is abhorrent to me.

So I will wait. For her to want me as much as I want her. She fears me, I tasted it on her skin when I first laid my suckers on her. I will not have her sweet scent polluted with it.

Drowning would be more palatable to me than hurting my treasure.

She shivers again and I bring her closer to my center, where she will hopefully find some sort of relief. We are still a ways from my palace and I will not have her freezing on me. Truth be told, as we move through the dark water the evening birds cawing overhead, her coloring only gets paler. Her fingers start turning blue as do her full lips, no longer that tasty red they were at her father's house.

I never realized what a cold life I led until now.

The chill of the water seeps into my own muscles. I would offer her my servant's clothing—my clothing—but they are both waterlogged. That would only add to her chill.

There is only one thing to do and hopefully, my sweet human will not hate me for it.

Gripping her fancy gown with my suckers I pull it from her body. The material tears away easily and I feast on the sight before me. Pale skin, glowing in the moonlight, freckles dotting her slender arms and shoulders. Her shift is thin and soaked, clinging like a second skin, I decide to leave her in this measly layer to preserve some of her modesty. The garment is translucent, her small, pale pink nipples pushing against the front. Try as I might I cannot stop my eyes from drifting lower to the shadowy place between her thighs.

My eyes can make out just a hint of red hair down there as well.

Even with my mouth watering I shake myself, pulling her even closer to me. My human stirs, letting out a soft moan and lifting her arms. They wrap around my neck as best as they can and she burrows into me. My tentacles encircle her legs and waist, trying to warm up as much of her as I can. My human shifts slightly and nuzzles in deep letting out another soft moan. My cock hardens against her and I grit my teeth as she slides against it.

We stay locked together like that for several moments. The soft sound of the waves lapping against the side of the boat, a slight breeze tugging at her hair. Being able to touch so much of her soft skin is making my head spin. I need to see all of her, to taste her pretty cunt, to shove myself so—

No, I will not give in to instinct. I will be patient with my treasure.

Her blue eyes blink up at me and she smiles softly, making this moment even better. The way she looks at me thinks that perhaps my lust is not just one-sided and that maybe—

"What the fuck!" She cries, her eyes flying wide and she pushes at me, trying to free herself from my hold. "Let go, get your tentacles off me! Why am I naked? Oh, gods...*oh gods*!"

I relax my grip on her slightly but not enough for her to get away. I'm still surrounding her but she can slide back from me and she does so immediately. Missing her warmth already, my tentacles fan out around her to make sure she doesn't try and slip into the water.

"Calm down before you tip us over."

"What is going on, where are we?" She swallows loudly. "Why did you undress me?"

That stench of fear invades my nostrils and I know I must reassure her, that this isn't what it looks like.

"You were cold, sweet one. I had to find some way to warm you or you would've frozen to death."

She opens her mouth to say something but then stops before springing into action. Turning to her side she begins to hoist herself up over the edge of the boat. My tentacles snap out gripping her around the waist once more and pulling her back in towards me. I ensnare her wrists and ankles so she is unable to move once more.

"Let me go, Kraken. Release me!"

"No," I say. She is never leaving me, someone would steal her, recognize what a treasure she is and take her from me. But they would not be careful with her, they would not treat her as the precious jewel she is. This human is *mine* and she will have to stay with me so I can make sure she is safe.

"You can't say no. Please, please, just let me go. Kill my father, he's the one you want."

"I want nothing of your father." My tentacle curls around her cheek, my suckers sticking to her soft skin and suctioning gently. She lets out a small gasp and begins to squirm again. I find I rather like her like this, restrained, mine completely for the taking. "You, my sweet one, are mine for eternity."

"It's not fair." Thrashing again, my little human tries to free herself from my grasp.

"Stop moving about like that, you will hurt yourself." My

tentacles curl tighter around her. "That would displease me greatly."

"I don't care what you want. Hear me, Kraken, the second I get free I will kill you. I will not be kept here."

"I like your spirit." And it is true, I do. She is lively and a challenge, one I will delight in bringing under my control. My human can say she hates and wants to kill me, but I can smell her. Her arousal scents the air, as sweet as honey, and I long for a taste of it. To taste her rage and fire, to feast on it between her legs.

The long boat comes to a halt, my human distracted me, I hadn't even realized we were close to the palace.

My Drowned Palace is lit with glowing shells and aquatic fish. Eels swim along the pathways or are trapped in jars to keep the inside lit. Half of it is completely sunken, allowing for easy access into the ocean, my true domain. I do not know how this came to be in my family but it has been our home for centuries.

A few servants are milling around the front: a woman who drowned herself by stuffing rocks in her pocket, a couple who got caught in a storm, and a fisherman who crashed into the side of a cliff. All of them turn to note our arrival and I growl, I do not want any of them to see my human while she is basically naked. Her flesh is only for me to see.

My treasure. Mine.

"Fetch her some warm clothes," I bark at my servant who scurries off.

I watch as my treasure takes in my palace. Her sea blue eyes absorb everything, scanning along the weathered grays rocks, to the great metal door that has rusted from exposure to sea air. The wild seagrass that grows out in front and the fish that swim around us, illuminating the black water below us. A small part of me is worried that it won't be up to her standard. The house I took her from was opulent to be sure, perhaps she will see this as beneath her?

I will just have to shower her in precious pearls and jewels if that is the case.

"Where are we?" she asks, softly. I note that she is no longer trying to escape and that pleases me greatly.

"We are at my home. The Drowned Palace, built on an alcove at the edge of *The Woods*, its wild magic was said to have helped the first Kraken King forge this place. Who had it before us I do not know, I assume some long-forgotten human king."

She nods and squares her shoulders as if preparing for battle. My cock hardens even further. "And how long am I to remain here for?"

"Forever. Your father stole from me. I took you as payment, you belong to me for eternity." Her small hands shove at my chest and I hold back my chuckle. Even as her little fist pound against me I barely feel it.

"How is any of this fair?" she cries.

"It is not. But the world is not fair."

"And what are you planning on doing with me?" That determined look settles over her soft features again. "What could I possibly do for you?"

"Isn't it obvious?" My tentacle skims down her face, snagging on her plump lips and gently pulling them apart. "You will be my bride. My human pleasure vessel that I will fill nightly with my seed. I will keep you warm and fed and wet, begging for me to pleasure you with my cock and tentacles."

Her mouth pops open and I'm tempted to sneak my tentacle in there again, to feel the warm, wetness of her tongue. A broken sound leaves her and then she starts to shake. At first, I think she is shivering again so I move to wrap her in my embrace but it is not the cold making her move in this way. She is laughing. Giggles are bubbling out of her like air pockets coming to the surface.

She tries to cover her mouth but her laughter gets louder, more uncontrolled.

"Doesn't that just figure." Before I can ask what she means, she throws an arm over her eyes and flops down on the boat bench, trapping a few of my tentacles under her shaking body. Not that I would dare move them.

My human keeps laughing, sitting up I see that tears have begun leaking from her eyes. The moisture courses down her cheeks and our eyes lock. Whatever she sees turns her chuckles into sobs. Her eyes grow red and she starts crying in earnest now, her body being wrecked by uncontrollable wailing.

I slide a tentacle over her cheek to catch some of the wetness. There is a new scent tainting her honeyed smell. The sharp, metallic bite of despair.

"It is alright, my treasure. Do not be scared, do not get upset."

I should tell her now that the barbaric practice of taking human brides is not what this is. A voice inside of me whispers that I should reassure her but I do not know how. Not when she is looking at me like that. So scared and vulnerable. Words will not soothe her so I must show her through action.

Wiping away her tears, I watch in horror as she goes pliant in my grasp. The fire that has lit her blue eyes is gone. The defiant set to her red brows has been smoothed out. She is limp, as lifeless as my drowned servants.

I do not like this. Taming her spirit is one thing. To be

able to tame that fire is what I crave, but to have her completely void of it...

This disturbs me, I must find a way to bring her spark back.

"Well, I'm basically naked already. Might as well get this over with." My horror grows as her face remains emotionless. I watch in shock as she reaches for the hem of her shift. No, not like this. I do not want her like this. My tentacles wrap around her wrist to stop her movements.

The first time I see her, see all of her, she will be willing. Her scent will not carry any notes other than arousal. I vow this in my heart.

With a sinking feeling, I realize that I must stay true to my purpose and protect her from anything that could cause her harm. Even if that something she believes is me.

I can be patient for my little human, I have to be.

"Not like this, sweet one. I will wait until you are willing." Relief floods her features and my stomach sours even more. Does she really hate the idea of me touching her that much? I suppose I could've been a little bit gentler in my approach when she asked me what I wanted her for.

"And what if I am never willing?" she asks carefully. I grit my teeth but I stay firm in my resolve.

"I have all of eternity to prove to you that I am worthy of sharing your bed."

My human is quiet for a moment and then opens her mouth but the sounds of footsteps make her stop and glance over.

The servants have arrived. I take the clothes from their outstretched hands, a warm wool dress and matching cloak and boots, and expand my form so that my human has privacy from prying eyes to change. I will myself not to sneak a glance and I don't. Within seconds, my human is dressed and exiting the boat.

She tightly curls the cloak around her, the muted brown in sharp contrast with the soft curls of her vibrant hair. My treasure is so beautiful, if I am lucky enough to just be able to look at her all day then that will be enough for me.

"Are you hungry?" I ask and her stomach growls at the question.

With one tentacle draped along her back, I guide her toward the palace. "Come, let us see what has been prepared for dinner."

As we make our way into my home, I reach out with one of my tentacles. It slithers up her back and curls a lock of her hair around it while I inhale her scent. This little human will give herself to me completely. From this moment forward everything I do is to ensure that one day she will desire me the way I already desire her.

I just hope that day is sooner than it seems.

3

MELODY

No one would ever accuse this underwater palace of being too lively.

Not with the servants all being half-rotted corpses, skin blue and damp, missing eyes, and bones eaten by some creature. The woman who'd brought me my plate of roasted fish was missing several fingerbones, her hollowed-out skin drug along the table as she set my meal down. I shiver at the thought.

My stomach turns at the memory of watching my captor tear into his raw salmon dinner. Devouring it with sharp teeth, swallowing it down whole. Descaling it with a wipe of his tentacles, eating the heads and fins and all.

We had eaten our meals in silence, truth be told I was too scared to say anything. Waking up on that boat, half-dressed, I had assumed the worst and I thank the gods that, while my captive seems keen on keeping me trapped here, he will not abuse me in that way at least. I thought for sure after we had finished our meals he would instruct me to go to his chambers but he did not.

Instead, that same servant that had given me my dinner

led me down a long damp hall. The walls were covered in shells and seaweed, my feet squelching along the wet carpet, before reaching this room. A room with a heavy door and a lock. Motioning me inside I saw that the room was mostly dry. With an ornately carved fireplace that already had a roaring fire burning in it.

The bed is carved in the same style with soft-looking blue sheets and a dozen pillows. My servant left a few moments ago after telling me fresh clothes would be brought tomorrow and asked me if I needed anything else. I dismissed her, not able to stomach looking at her macabre form.

I feel bad for my reaction to all of them, after all, they are trapped here just the same as me.

This room is nice but I am no less a prisoner. Brought here by that creature and proclaimed to be his bedmate for eternity. Still, try as I might I cannot hate him for it. I should, I really should. Make no mistake, I am angry, but I have been so angry for so long it is buried so deep beneath the surface I can hardly reach for it anymore.

My governess had quite a time, trying to teach me to be a proper lady. To be poised and polite. To smile and make myself small and quiet, something all men of good breeding loved in a future wife. Those strong emotions I felt so fiercely as a child were not permitted and thus all of them were buried deep inside me.

Especially my growing resentment towards my father.

He is the one I should blame. This creature took me from an unpleasant life. Here I have been afforded all the comforts I could want. Despite the dress ripping, he has been kind to me. Gentle with his touches even though I can tell he desires more. Would a human man be as understanding?

Any human man that my father had wed me to would've demanded I open my legs to him without a second thought. To get pregnant and produce his heirs. At least my captor, the Kraken, wants to wait until I desire him. That earns him a little bit of redemption in my eyes.

Perhaps it is the shock of the evening, the way in which my world has just been turned upside down but I cannot seem to process what I am feeling. Besides the anger, there is curiosity. Maybe once he trusts me a bit more he will let me go exploring. Maybe I can live out my days an untouched virgin, kept by a sea creature, and be able to explore the grounds and take up a new hobby.

While it may not be the freedom I envisioned for myself it is better than the life I would've lived at home.

There is a darker part of me though. One that recalls what it felt like to be surrounded by him, sucked into the warm, slick mass of his muscles and tentacles. To be held so tightly and overpowered. It had made me wet between my legs, a fact that I would rather die than admit to him. When his tentacle had grazed my lips I had wanted him to push it into my mouth, like he had before I fainted. To push it past my teeth and tongue and keep going until...

Until I don't know what.

It is a dark desire, one I am not ready to confront yet. He is my captor. He is a creature of the sea and I should be repulsed by him. So why am I not? Why does the thought of him holding me down and restraining me, have my nipples pressing into the front of my gown?

Have I finally found the one thing that has alluded me? A male who does not want a meager woman who has nothing to say for herself and lets him completely control her with no resistance. Males who called me half-wild and said I was unfit to wed when they thought I couldn't hear.

They were right, I was unfit to wed some sniveling lord like them. Why were they worthy of my submission? Even my attention?

The Kraken did not like it when I put my mask on in front of him. When I fell back on those lessons and became sullen and pliant. He hated it. He said he liked my spirit and now in the mix of all those emotions I am feeling, a small glimmer of hope is snaking its way through me as well.

Needing to distract myself from these thoughts, and from the boredom settling in, I warm myself one last time by the fire and exit the room.

My new boots stomp along the dank carpet, the hallway illuminated in a soft blue light. Glowing eels are trapped in jars along the walls, swimming back and forth to highlight the path. Shells and starfish glow as well, showing off the rotted wood of the walls. Some old portraits that were once mounted to the wall have been torn and shriveled up. Who owned this castle before it became the Kraken's home? His theory of it being an old human king looks to be correct.

The air carries salty notes of the sea, I can hear distant splashing. Being so close to the water, I am shocked that it isn't muggier. No, if anything the air is crisp and fresh, less polluted than the air of the city I was living in. It reminds me of the air at our cottage along the sea.

Nostalgia tightens my throat but I walk on.

The water at my feet is getting deeper, sneaking up to my ankles and soaking the hem of my gown. The water is cool, less frigid than the open ocean I experienced when we first arrived here. The hallway thins and more creatures begin to glow until I realize the walls of the hallway have faded away. In front of me is a small lagoon, a few glittering fish swim through the shallow water, lily pads glow the same color as the moon above, and night-blooming flowers perfume the air.

It is truly magical and I edge my way toward it. Perhaps this will be my new hobby, exploring my new home. Finding what treasures have lurked here for centuries and cataloging them.

I kneel down near the edge, my dress soaking through, and gently finger one of the plants. It curls around my finger and releases an even more intoxicating scent. My eyes catch on movement below, three of the most gorgeous fish I have ever seen swim towards me. They are a torrent of brightly colored scales. Blues, pinks, golds, and silvers all streak through the water, glittering and inviting.

They have mesmerized me so much that I do not even realize I am being stalked.

An eel with oily black scales and even darker eyes has slithered through the water. Those fathomless eyes lock on me and by the time I spy its movements, it has already struck, wrapping its body around my wrist and yanking me forward.

Down into the dark water below.

I manage to scream just before I was pulled under, my mouth and lungs filled with salty water. The temperature of the water is a shock. Even as I thrash, the creature's grip on me is too strong, I can't fight it. I am going to die, there is no way for me to survive this.

We rip through the water. Bubbles fly passed me at the speed we are going. My eyes burn so I close them, it is not like I can see much of anything anyway. Lungs burning, I make peace with my final moments in the world of the living.

Suddenly there is a shift.

A hum of power radiates through the water so overwhelming even the eel pauses its movements. With the last of my strength, I peel my eyes open and am met with a terrifying sight. Glowing red eyes are coming towards me, faster than lightning.

Blue tentacles unfurl towards me and rip me from the creatures grasp. I watch in horror as the eel is wrapped in the Kraken's limb and squeezed and squeezed and...popped. His insides floating around me.

I should be disturbed and alarmed, but I find that I am only aroused. Again, I will blame this on the lack of oxygen. My brain is shutting down, it is the only logical explanation.

The next thing I know is that I am being ripped toward the surface. The tentacles push me the final distance before we break through. I suck down lungfuls of air, coughing and spitting up salt water.

Gently, I am slid back onto the safety of the shore, the glowing plants of the lagoon finally coming into focus. My chest is rising and falling so fast, and my wet hair is plastered to my face just like my dress is to my body.

The salty taste of the water still lingers in my mouth and burns my eyes. It is only by some miracle, I survived this.

My miracle is hanging at the edge of the water. He's shed semi-human form. The Kraken is just a mass of meaty tentacles and a round head with those glowing red eyes. His mouth is parted slightly and I can make out a few sharp teeth.

I should be disgusted and repulsed but I am not. When looking at him, I find that I am only grateful that he got to me in time. One of his tentacles lay by my side and I gently grasp it in my hand. It pulses with life, the suckers attaching to my palm in a firm press.

"What happened out here, sweet one?"

My hand squeezes his limb gently, curiously. I hear him

let out a low moan but I cannot stop touching him. The tentacle is smooth and slick. Something other than water coats it in a fine, oily sheen. I wonder what that substance would feel like on my own body. My arms, my legs, my breasts...

"That eel grabbed me. I was exploring the lagoon and it just attacked me. If you hadn't gotten to me in time..." I don't need to finish the sentence, we both know what would've happened.

"My palace is not safe. Especially for someone like you." I crawl towards him on my hands and knees until we are face to face at the edge of the lagoon. "If you wish to go exploring tell me and I will keep you safe."

Smiling slightly I nod. I want to thank him for saving me but then I remember something. Something that I should've asked hours before now.

"I'm Melody, by the way. I should've asked earlier, but what is your name? I assume you were not born, Kraken of the Darksea?" I ask.

He is quiet for a moment and I fear he is not going to tell me but then he opens his mouth.

"My name is Zalenyk, sweet one. No one has called me that in centuries."

"Zalenyk." I like the way it tastes on my tongue. His tentacles shiver at my utterance of it, he seems to like me saying it as well. "Zalenyk you saved me."

I like the way he looks at me. The protective way in which some of his tentacles still hold me. Like the threat to my safety is still present, that he is the only one who can keep me safe. And I truly believe that he is.

To be so utterly desired is something I have never experienced.

My oxygen-deprived brain decides that is all the reason

we need. Leaning forward towards his massive form I brush my mouth over his. I've never kissed anyone before but I am sure whatever technique I used with a human man would've needed adjustment to kiss a Kraken anyways.

Zalenyk is frozen. His mouth is unmoving as my lips meet his cool, slick ones. I pull back slightly, self-consciousness seeping in, causing me to question if I've just embarrassed myself.

Then he moves.

All at once his massive body is over the side of the lagoon and I am being consumed. His mouth is on mine kissing me with renewed vigor. His tentacles tangle in my hair, around my waist and arms, gripping me tightly, rubbing me up and down. That oil substance coats my mouth and it is as crisp as the evening air.

My pussy is obscenely wet, the moisture running down along my thighs I know has very little to do with the water I was just pulled from.

One of his suckers grazes my nipple still covered in my gown and I moan. He uses the opportunity to push his tongue into my mouth. The warm wet muscle dances with my own, fighting with mine as his tentacle moves back and forth against my breast.

I shiver and I'm not sure if it is from my damp clothes or the assault he is having on my sense. This is wrong, in so many ways, but I can't find it in myself to stop. Or to care for that matter. This has stoked a fire in me; he has stoked a fire in me.

I'll do anything I can to keep it roaring.

A particularly strong shake passes through me and Zalenyk halts his movements.

"You are cold, sweet Melody. Come let us go inside, I must get you warm."

Crying out, I desperately want his tentacle back on my breast.

"Warm me yourself," I gasp, trying to capture his mouth again.

He growls in answer. Somehow when he had first come over the ledge of the lagoon, my legs had opened to accommodate his massive size. Now that we have stopped kissing, I can still feel his tentacles coasting up and down my gown-soaked legs. Tentatively grazing the sensitive skin of my inner thighs. A few of them have slid beneath my hem, inching higher to the most intimate part of me.

They are careful as if seeking my permission.

I nod my head and smash my lips against his again.

A tentacle grazes my slick folds and I cry out. The sensation is hot and cold, firm yet soft. It is an exploring touch, one that causes more moisture to leak out of me.

"Wetter than a rainstorm, my treasure. Are you ready to let me have you this way?" Zalenyk asks.

Despite the immense amount of lust, I am feeling, his question clears some of it from my head. Am I ready to have him inside me? To lose my virginity like this? With him?

"I do not know if I am ready for everything," I say carefully. "But I would like to do some exploring. With you. I don't know much of anything really, all I know is that you feel good"

"Have you ever been with a man, sweet one?" I shake my head now, a blush warming my cheeks. A shutter racks him and the tentacle grazing my folds presses down harder, the sucker suctioning onto a little bundle of nerves, and my back arches, a scream pulled from my lips.

I've touched myself before but nothing like this. I overheard one of our servants say the stable boy did something like this with his mouth on her clit but I cannot imagine it felt anything like this.

"We will explore each other, Melody. And once you are comfortable with me, you will let me have you."

Two tentacles tangle in the top of my gown and tug gently, asking if he can remove it for me. I'm so overwhelmed by the sensation all I can do is nod my head again. In a moment the gown is shredded, my thin shift the only thing between us.

"You are pink and pretty everywhere, little human."

I see now what he was doing, a torrent of tentacles underneath the hem of my undergarments. Some are wrapped around my ankles holding my legs apart, keeping them open even as I try to close them as his sucker works my clit again. It's too much.

"Do not hide your pretty cunt from me when I seek to pleasure it." Another tentacle comes up and circles around my hole gently, my whole body tenses as I wait for the intrusion. "Not tonight, sweet one, but soon. Soon you will beg for my cock to fill you. To have all your holes stuffed with me, and trust when I say I will not deny you that honor."

More moisture leaks out of me and flows down through the cheeks of my ass.

I can hear the slick slide of his tentacles through me as he returns his attention to my clit. That substance he has been secreting only adds to the wetness. My gown is pushed up and slowly my naked skin comes into view. Freckles dot along my bare stomach, and my nipples are pale and peaked under his gaze. The growl he emanates causes all his tentacles to vibrate adding even more pleasure.

Here I am, being held open by this creature and all I can do is wait for my orgasm to decimate me. It had always taken me a while to find completion with my hand but

Zalenyk has already mastered my body. A few more rubs of my clit and I will be done for.

"Zalenyk, I'm—"

"Close?"

"Yes!" I scream, his tentacle sucking on me with a new intensity. My toes curl and my head is thrown back. His tentacles wrap around my arm and my throat, not choking me but making sure I know who is in control here. He keeps sucking on me and his mouth swoops down to kiss me once more. Zalenyk's tongue slips into my mouth and I'm panting, my hips writhing in time with his tentacle.

"Come for me, Melody. When you do it scream my name so all the fish in the sea can hear who pleasures this little pussy."

I'm powerless to do anything else.

My orgasm takes me to a high that is almost painful. Muscles flexing, I clench down around nothing as wave after wave of euphoria hits me. It's too much, this creature… no Zalenyk has broken me. Ruined using my own hand for me because I surely could never replicate this.

"Zalenyk, Zalenyk." Babbling his name incoherently he only chuckles, realizing the tight hold along my limbs. His form sneaks down my body, those red eyes looking up at me over the mound of my pussy.

The smile on my face is small.

"Let me taste it, let me find out if you are just as sweet here as I imagine you are."

"Whatever you want." The words are barely out before I feel his tongue lick up my center. He laps at me, and attacks my clit, sucking on it the way his suckers did. Two tentacles come up to attack my breasts, squeezing the mounts before the suckers attach to my nipples and begin sucking on them as well.

My body is quickly being brought to another peak.

I fear this orgasm may actually be the one to break me. Zalenyk rubs his face in my wetness, his own wetness mingling with mine and heightening my sensations.

"I am marking you in my scent, sweet one. That way, anyone who gets close enough to smell you knows I will kill them for touching you. For attempting to take what is mine."

That thought warms me, a funny feeling settling in my stomach. My legs are hoisted up by his tentacles. They push them back towards my chest so I am on full display for him. He licks from my asshole to my pussy in one clean sweep that has me moaning even louder.

"Come again, come now."

Further solidifying his control over my body, I do so on command. Violently, my body goes up in flames once more. I thrash in his grip, screaming his name as I come and Zalenyk is there. His tentacles hold me through it as he feasts between my legs.

Drinking down every drop of my pleasure.

I do not know what occurred here tonight, but one thing is sure. Zalenyk is a creature to me no more. I no longer want to escape him but to get closer to him, to feel him within me. If I could move I would suggest we go the whole way tonight but that last orgasm has me spent.

My eyes turn heavy. With one last kiss to my pussy, Zalenyk slips up my body once more and wraps me in a warm cocoon of his tentacles.

He licks his lips, a smile playing on them. "Your cunt is delicious."

I bark a laugh and my face heats. This Kraken, Zalenyk, also seems to be the only being I've ever felt shy around. He seems to know that and revels in it.

"Come now little one, let me put you to bed."

There is a faint metallic smell of magic and suddenly I am being carried by two very strong human arms. Zalenyk's steps are sturdy as he marches me back into the castle. His tentacles have shrunk to be beard size and they stroke over my cheek.

I fight to stay awake but as he settles me onto the bed, stripping me out of my wet shift, I find that I am losing the battle. The room is deliciously hot and I sink into the plush mattress. Zalenyk covers me with the comforter and steps back from the bed.

"I will see you in the morning, Melody." He turns on his heel and makes for the door.

Let him leave, you need sleep and time to think about what happened out there. Time to think about escaping. I should listen to those thoughts, should turn into the warmth of this bed, and let this night fade away like sugar in water.

I should do all of those things but I don't.

"Wait," I call, Zalenyk freezes on the threshold. Turning to me, I pull back the comforter and pat the bed beside me. "Stay with me. Hold me while I sleep, this place is new to me and you..." *Don't say it.* "I like being near you"

To admit such weakness causes me to close my eyes. Surely he will be like every other man and use this need as a bargaining chip. To exploit it for their own gain.

Zalenyk is quiet and I look up at him, he gestures toward the fire, his blue human arm glowing in the light.

"The fire is painful to me. I cannot sleep exposed to that much heat, but I want you comfortable above all else."

"You can keep me warm better than any fire." *What is happening to me?*

"Are you sure?"

Am I sure? Yes.

For the first time in a long time, I let go. Those doubts I had a moment ago, I decide to let fade. They were born from a life my father stole for me to have. A life I never truly wanted. In his own way, albeit perhaps not the most selfless act, Zalenyk gave me my freedom back. There are no rules with him, no tricks.

I refuse to live with my mask and guard up any longer.

"Stay with me, Zalenyk. I want you to."

Rushing water sounds from behind him and my Kraken catches it in his hand. It is a small bubble of water that he tosses into the fire. The fireplace goes out with a sizzle and plunges the room into darkness. His footsteps are light on the carpet as the bed dips under his weight.

I must admit he is easier to cuddle in this form.

Sliding on my side, I throw my leg over his middle and curl my arm around his neck. His arms come up to circle my back, tracing his fingers down my arm, my spine. All the while his tentacles tangle in my hair.

Feeling safe and relaxed I close my eyes and feel his rhythmic breathing, letting it seep into my bones and soothe me.

"You are the most precious thing in the world to me, Melody. You do not know the gift you have just given me, to let me hold you like this."

That decides me then and there. I will lean into what this is between Zalenyk and me. I owe it to him and myself to make a real go at this life here.

With that thought in mind, I give in and sink into the familiar waters of *sleep*.

4

ZALENYK

My Melody is beyond compare.

There are no words that can describe her. No words are worthy of her. It is not enough for me to keep her safe and treasured in my care, not after last night. No, I must win her affection and her kindness. Her desire. Her love.

It is apparent to me that she desires the responses I can coax from her body. Her thighs could not have been more eager and I can still feel her slender thighs squeezing the sides of my head. Her honeyed taste dripped on my tongue as my tentacles coasted over, squeezing every ounce of her delicious skin on display.

I must win Melody over, to show her that her place is here with me, that I will do anything to make her blue eyes sparkle. To have her look at me, not in fear, but in reverence knowing I'm the only one worthy enough to pleasure her.

And I have set about doing that this morning.

We sit at the breakfast table and I watch with fiendish joy as every type of fish is brought in and sat down in front of my human. Salmon, rainbow fish, and shellfish that live deep below the surface, are all plated and presented to her as an offering. The sailors may worship me but I worship Melody and I always will.

This morning had been a first for me. While I have had lovers in the past, none of which I will ever recall now that I have Melody. I had never felt this overwhelming sense of rightness as I did when I woke up this morning. She had held on to me throughout the night, her soft skin fitting against my muscles. Deliciously warm, my tentacles had traced her cheeks and eyelids, committing each freckle to memory.

Melody's blue eyes had blinked open, wary and unsure, her cheeks staining pink. My fiery human is shy in the morning light. Hopefully, she is recalling what it felt like to have me feasting on her pink cunt. I want her to think about that for the rest of her days.

Before I could ask if I could eat her for breakfast, however, a servant came in to deliver Melody fresh clothing. Human clothes aren't in great supply here but I should be fixing that shortly. In the warm glow of the morning, I pressed a kiss to her forehead and told her to join me for breakfast.

I'll cherish the soft smile she gave me for the rest of my life.

While her body is a treat, I want to know about her. To show her that she is safe with me, to be who she is. That I will not keep her trapped. My human is adventurous and I have something planned for her this morning that I think she will really enjoy.

Unfortunately for me, it does not look like she is enjoying her breakfast at the moment.

"What's wrong, Melody? Is the fish not to your liking? I wanted you to have a wide variety so I could learn your favorites." If she hates all of these I will simply have to go out and catch her more. Rare fishes that seek to evade even me.

She is more than worth the hassle if only for her to smile at me again.

"No, these are wonderful. You are too generous...it's just that..." My sweet human squirms in her seat, a blush rising to her cheeks. She doesn't wish to tell me but I will have no secrets between us.

"Tell me, my treasure. Whatever it is you can tell me."

Wrinkling her freckled nose, she grimaces. "I'm not the biggest fan of fish."

Not a fan of fish? Oh, my sweet human. I must fix this at once. She will want for nothing under my care.

"I am sorry, Melody. I did not know." I call for my servants, who appear in the doorway of the dining room. "I will fix this at once. Make sure human food is found, in addition to new clothes. Do you have any preferences, sweet one?"

"Um," she hums, thinking. "For breakfast, bacon if you can find it. If not, my mother used to make oatcakes, it's quite simple. I can even make them if you can find the ingredients."

"I will cook these oatcakes for you, you will not be made to work in my care." She giggles at my words but one look at my face lets her know I am serious. It is my honor to wait on her hand and foot. To provide her with whatever she needs.

"Zalenyk, I don't mind really."

Dismissing my servants with a wave of my tentacles, I have Melody's plate taken away. The room grows quiet as I sulk over what I've done. Not even a day and already my sweet one is going hungry under my roof.

"So," Melody says, interrupting my thoughts. "Will you show me around the palace today?"

In a second my mood is lifted as I remember my plan.

"Yes, I have something to show you that I think will please you."

"You already seem to know how to do that quite well," Melody responds, a small smile curving her lips. Already there is a change in her, and it warms me to know that I had some part of it. When I brought her here she was scared and sad but underneath all of that was a fire, one I can tell she had been suppressing for years. That icy facade of hers is slowly being melted away and I wonder how much more of a treasure she will be when it is all gone.

"When someone is in possession of a treat such as yourself, it would be wrong not to enjoy it."

"But you didn't...enjoy yourself. It was me who got all the...pleasuring."

"You don't think it pleases me to make you come?" She looks away, her face hot. I extend out a tentacle and wrap it around her chin, pulling her back to face me. "You don't think getting to feast on your sweet pussy, to drink down your pleasure, gives me pleasure in turn? To know that I am the only one who's seen you that way. Touched you that way. It makes me feel like a god."

"You are already a god," she points out.

"No, little human. Men may have called me one, but I became one last night with your come dripping off of my chin and your scream of my name ringing in my ears."

"Does that make me a god too? Since I had the power to make you one."

"I'll worship you like one." Her teeth sink into her plump lower lip, I can smell her honeyed scent becoming richer. My little human is wet, just like she should always be around me.

Tossing back her long mane of red hair, she leans her elbows on the table.

"So how did you actually become the Kraken of the Darksea?"

So curious, my Melody.

"My father was the Kraken before me. When he died centuries ago I inherited this place and his powers. There used to be more of my kind, but most of them fled deeper into the ocean. Into their own aquatic kingdoms along the ocean floor." My mouth twists into a grin. "But someone had to stay here and watch over the humans. To keep them in line and that task fell to me."

"Must be lonely, being the only one of your kind left."

"It's not so bad." Melody raises a scarlet brow at me. "Besides, I am not alone now. If more of my kind still existed here I'd have to kill them all to keep you."

Her mouth pops open. "Kill them? Why?"

My laugh is dark, my tentacle tracing over her lips.

"They get one smell of your sweetness in the water and they would want to take you from me. To claim you as their own. You are mine, Melody. Anyone who seeks to take you will wish for death."

Her chest rises and falls, nipples pressing against the wool material of her brown gown. She likes the idea, of belonging to me, her body already knows it. Knows that it is mine, that it belongs to me.

"You want me that much?"

"I need you that much."

"Why?"

"Why?" I echo. "You are a treasure, Melody. Your bastard father should've seen it. Should've protected you and kept you safe but he didn't. I will not make the same mistake."

A harsh shiver passes through Melody, whether from the chill in the air or something else makes no difference to me. It is time to show her my surprise.

"I thought I might take you to the hot spring. It's located just over here and the water will warm you." Melody's mouth opens in a wide grin and she claps her hands lightly. Warmth unfurls within me that I have pleased her.

"That sounds wonderful. I have been in need of a bath."

She takes my offered tentacle and I wrap it around her waist. Pulling her up against my side I lead her from the dining room. It is a short journey to the hot spring, as we walk through the palace I keep her close, casting warning growls at any of my servants whose gaze lingers on her too long.

Melody is mine, only mine.

Through the back of the castle, there is an opening to the spring. Already the air has turned muggy, as white steam billows over the lip of the pool. There is a riot of brightly colored flowers and plants dotting the sides of the spring, I hope that they please my sweet human. She deserves beautiful things.

"Zalenyk this is incredible," Melody says, stepping away from my side to investigate the spring closer. Always so curious.

"I thought you would like it. This will also warm you up, especially when we get into the colder months. The water is so hot, no other creatures can stand it besides me so you should be safe in here."

Melody nods, her blue eyes unfocused as she stares at the pool.

I watch as she begins to undress and my mouth goes dry.

While I already have had my mouth and tentacles on every part of her body, seeing it on display like this in the morning sun unlocks something inside me. Her heavy wool gown is cast aside, and the long mane of her red hair drapes down her back. Next goes her thin shift, leaving me to feast on the sight of her smooth back, down to the pert little cheeks of her ass.

There's a freckle just at her hip and I want to lick it. To memorize every single one and kiss them all until she squirms.

As if hearing my thoughts she turns, her red lips tilted in a small smile. I can just see a hint of her breast and I growl as she turns back and jumps into the spring. Warm water goes everywhere and I hurry to join her. Her redhead resurfaces and she holds on to the side of the spring.

The water is shallow over here but Melody is tiny, of course, she cannot stand.

Reaching out one of my tentacles, I suction to her waist and hold her aloft.

"Thank you, it's been a while since I've been swimming. I fear I am not as good at it as I used to be."

"Do you like to swim?" I ask, hungry to know if this is something we can do together in the future.

"I loved it as a girl. To tell you the truth Zalenyk, I was a bit of a wild child. If you thought you captured a lady, I'm afraid you'd be mistaken." Melody laughs but there is no joy in it. She dips her chin and I use another tentacle to tilt her head back up so I can look into her eyes.

"Melody you're perfect. I want you, not a lady, you. I knew it from the moment I saw you." My sweet human opens her mouth as if to argue but I cut her off. "Tell me more about you as a girl."

"Oh! Well..." she trails off, "we were poor. Even as a

child, I knew that. We barely had anything to eat, even before my mother died things were hard. But we had love. So much of it that I wonder if my father also bargained away some of his soul that day in *The Woods.* My mother was the heart of our family and she encouraged me to be free, to run, and have fun. To be curious and adventurous."

"She sounds wonderful," I say and Melody rewards me with another smile.

"She was wonderful. She would tell me stories about you, you know? The cautionary tales of not swimming in dark water, which I had a fondness for as a child. My mother believed in the legends and said they were real. If she could see me now, I think she wouldn't find this situation odd in the slightest, just smug that she had always been right about your existence."

Her blue eyes go a little damp and my grip tightens on her. Using my tentacle at her chin, I wipe away a few stray tears that have leaked out. My sweet Melody, so lonely and lost, not so unlike myself.

But I have found her now and she will never feel that way again.

"What about you? Where's your mother?"

"My mother is..." I search for the right words but none come. My mother? I hardly remember her. "She died. Shortly after I was born."

"Oh Zalenyk, I'm so sorry."

"She was human," I say carefully and watch Melody's eyes fly open.

"Human?" she asks.

"Yes, Krakens cannot breed with each other, so it used to be commonplace to steal a human bride in order to get her with child."

"Is that why you stole me? To further your line?" her voice is small, and she won't look at me.

"No, Melody. That is not the reason." I slide closer to her in the water, my tentacles latching onto her arms and legs in a gentle hold. Forcing her to look up at me I let her see the truth in my eyes. "My father loved my mother. Loved her more than anything in this world. When he took her to be his underwater bride she was so frightened, and he realized he could not harm her. Could not sit back as tradition carried on. Our kind would be better than pulling unwilling women under the water in order to procreate with them."

"So what happened?"

"He outlawed the practice and our race slowly died off. I'm one of the last Krakens, Melody. I intend to keep it that way."

"And if I wanted a child? Wanted a child between us?"

Her question throws me. She would want a child? My child.

"When you're ready to finally let me have you, finally ready to let me plant myself so deep inside of you that I soak you with my seed, then we can talk about having a child." I curl a lot of her red hair around my tentacle. "For now, let me show you something. Do you trust me?"

Despite our conversation topic, she nods without pause. Still wrapped in my tentacles, I lead her away from the edge of the pool and deep down into it. Melody's warm naked body is pressed into mine, her nipples hard as they graze over my flesh.

I want to suck them, bite them, and play with them but that will all have to wait.

We go deeper beneath the surface and I watch her start to get nervous, quickly losing air in her lungs. Summoning some of my magic I cast it forward, creating a Melody-sized air bubble rich in oxygen. The pocket covers her and the tentacles I hold her with.

Melody sucks down lungfuls of air and her eyes grow wide as she takes in the sights.

"Zalenyk, what is this?"

"I can do a few tricks here and there, sweet one. Would you like to explore more of the spring?"

"Yes!" Excitement colors her words, my curious little one. I knew she would be eager.

So together, with my treasure wrapped tightly in my embrace, we swim the depths of the spring. At this depth, the water is cooler, so there are a few schools of fish that pass us. Their scales glittering in the faint light. Melody runs her hand along a few waving locks of seaweed that passes us by. Our bare feet drag along the sandy bottom.

The deeper we go the darker it gets. I can see her perfectly, her eyes wide inside her air bubble, taking everything in. When she is completely unable to see she grips my tentacle, holding on to me as if I am a lifeline.

Like she trusts me to keep her safe.

I can feel Melody begin to sag in my arms and I know she is tired. With one last push, we make our way back up to the spring and break through the surface. Her air pocket is popped and she leans against the lip of the pool. Chest rising and falling out of the water, her pale pink nipples coming in and out of view.

Her expression is carefree, her guard finally gone for the first time since I brought her here. That mask has been smashed and I am seeing the real Melody. Gods, she is so beautiful.

We are quiet for a few moments, basking in the warmth of the sun and in each other's company. My tentacle traces up and down her spine, tangling in her hair, and sucking on her shoulders.

"What if I'm ready now? For more," she says, quietly.

My heart stops beating, and time around me slows.

"Are you sure?" I ask my grip on her tightening involuntarily. She nods, her blue eyes bright and trusting.

In the water, we move closer, as if our bodies have given up fighting even the smallest distance between us. Her red hair floats around her and her ruby lips part, waiting, inviting me in to taste them. I'll taste every bit of her, right here right now—

Footsteps sound behind us, and Melody gasps.

Covering her completely with my body, I turn, ready to strangle whoever dares to interrupt us. A couple of my servants rush in, their milky eyes are unblinking. This one had a particularly gruesome death, with half his face missing from being smashed against a cliff before drowning. The words that leave his mouth are garbled.

"Your Majesty, the merchant ship you requested we find has been secured. We are unloading all of their cargo now. It was on course for a human lord and his family so it is filled with all the human things you required."

"Stealing? Really?" Melody chastises me but I see her amused small smile.

"Only the best for you, sweet one." A giggle burst from her lips and I want to drink the sound. Before I get the chance there is a loud ruckus from inside the palace. A few curses and shouts make my servant grimace.

"The captain and his crew of the vessel were not...easy to subdue."

Another sharp yell sounds and Melody pulls on my tentacle to get my attention.

"Seems like we better go and investigate."

I nod solemnly and dismiss my servant. As much as I would love to sink into her right now in this pool, I will not be able to focus until I know that these sailors do not pose a threat to her. I will dispatch them by any means necessary to keep them away from my treasure.

My treasure...who I help rise from the hot spring and watch as she dresses. It is agony watching her naked skin being taken away from me. Even after I had this ship captured in hopes they had fresh clothes for Melody a secret part of me wishes I could burn them all and force her to walk around naked.

However, that would mean my servants may also see her body, and then I would have to drown them all. Again.

Tucking into my side we make our way back into the palace, Melody's damp hair curling and tickly my face. The shouting gets louder until we come into the front room. The captain, an older man with graying hair and wrinkled skin, is already gagged and restrained on the floor. There is blood trickling from his temple indicating some sort of altercation took place.

His crew of five other men looks in the same condition.

One look at me and their eyes widen, fresh sweat breaking out along their brow. It seems they know me and my reputation.

"It may be best to leave them like this and let the tide take them, Your Majesty," one of my servants says. "No loose ends, since they know the location of this place."

The humans on the floor crying out around their gags. Thrashing on the floor. I nod my head, that would be the easiest course of action.

"No, Zalenyk," Melody says at my side. "Do not kill them. Not for just doing their job. You're not the monster of those legends. We'll take their cargo but spare their lives."

"Melody, you don't understand, I can't just let them—"

"Please spare them," she whispers, her small hand coasting down my front, dangerously close to my hard cock. She knows it too, the little siren. Melody rubs her breasts along my side, her lips tickling the short tentacles of my beard. "Please, for me."

Her hand continues its torture. Rubbing all over me, letting her tongue trace along a tentacle. I groan brokenly, she does not fight fair.

"Fine, sweet one. I will spare them. For you and only for you. " Clearing my throat I dismiss the human men.

"Your Majesty, do you wish to see the items recovered?"

I only wish to sink my cock so deep into Melody's tight cunt that there would be no way to pull us apart.

However, that will have to wait. I need to make sure she has everything she could ever want. To prove to her that giving me a chance was not a mistake and that I will make sure she wants for nothing.

Melody must see how conflicted I am because she presses up on her toes and kisses my cheek. Her lips are warm and smooth and I instantly want them back.

"Check on everything, I'll see you at dinner." Melody's smile widens and her eyes become twin blue flames. "And then tonight we'll do more exploring. On land this time."

Turning from the room she doesn't see my tentacles expand and reach after her. Wishing to drag her back to my side and hold her and keep her. Already I miss her but this task is important.

Tonight, I will have my treasure in every way imaginable.

5

MELODY

Despite the feast before me, I find I'm not that hungry.

Well, that is for food at least. Lust has stolen my appetite, but I know I will need my energy for what is to come. Taking bite after bite, I tuck into my meal. It really is no hard feat when there are perfectly cooked chunks of beef swimming in rich wine sauces. Fluffy mashed potatoes and roasted vegetables. Stealing is wrong and uncalled for but I cannot deny that it warmed my heart that Zalenyk went through all of this trouble for me.

I take a sip of my wine, my belly full, and look at my dinner companion who tears into another raw piece of fish.

Did I think him hideously ugly before? Surely not. There's more to Zalenyk than meets the eye. Mainly how caring and protective he is of me. I can still hear the growl he leveled at the human captain who came up to retrieve some food for him and his men. The way his eyes lingered on me for too long.

Zalenyk stopped it, something not even my father could've claimed to do.

Maybe that's the cause of these feelings inside of me, the ones only he is able to stir. The protectiveness, the care, the understanding. All of the things I've been missing out on for so long. Zalenyk fulfills those needs and these new ones I am experiencing.

As if he can feel my eyes on him he looks up from his plate and tilts his head.

"Is the food pleasing to you, my sweet one?"

"Yes, it's delicious. That was the only good thing about my father's new wealth." I laugh without humor. "My health improved greatly after being on the brink of starvation for so long."

"Never again," Zalenyk vows, "will you want for anything. I promise."

My thighs grow damp.

"I know."

"I wish to learn," he pauses, "more about your life after your father's bargain."

I take another sip of wine. This conversation is uncomfortable but Zalenyk looks at me so honestly, it is clear he just wants to know as much as possible about me. That thought allows me to clear my suddenly dry throat.

"Initially, I was happy. My father was still my father in those early days, only now we had the means to actually enjoy the comforts of life. We were happy, before it all, but living hand to mouth can take a lot out of even the happiest of people."

Zalenyk nods and I continue.

"I believed his wealth would afford me some sort of freedom, girls in our old village were being married off at the age I was. This new rise in station meant I would be educated, and we had the means to travel something my mother had always wanted to do, but it became apparent that my future was not mine after all. Especially after the first lord remarked on how lovely of a young woman I was. That was when my father began to change. The wealth had changed him into someone greedy and now he saw me as a new way to gain more wealth."

The growl that comes from across the table shakes the table. A tentative tentacle reaches out to brush against my cheek.

"And now, I've trapped you here." There is a note of self-loathing in his tone. I should agree, tell him that yes my prison has changed from my father's home to his drowned palace but that doesn't seem right. Zalenyk has been kind to me in his own way and helped me explore things I would've never seen before.

"It's not the same, Zalenyk. Not anymore at least," I say but his brow remains furrowed. "Will you show me the world? Take me on adventures, show me the sea that you rule over?"

"Yes." His answer is immediate. "Whatever you wish I will give to you."

"Then perhaps it is a good thing you took me. Lest I become a breeding mare to a cruel, aging prince who thinks the best thing about me is that I can provide him, with children." Taking another sip of wine, I look Zalenyk directly in the eye. "Why did you take me, Zalenyk? Why didn't you just kill my father outright?"

"Because" —he hesitates— "when I saw you there, so beautiful and afraid, I realized you were mine. Something inside me clicked and I knew I had to have you. Perhaps it was years of tradition that even I wasn't immune to but I had to take you. Make you my bride. You feared me, yes, but you weren't disgusted by me. Beneath all of that, I saw you, your fire, and I knew I had to claim it for myself."

"Most men don't like my fire."

"I do. I want to feast on it between your legs, to have it glow in your eyes when I'm inside you."

My thighs clench together, my nipples hard and chafing against my gown.

"There are so many things that I want to give you, sweet one. So many ways in which I want to claim you I don't know which one I want to do first."

"We can do all of them," I say, my voice rough.

"Are you sure?"

"Yes."

I don't know where this boldness comes from but it has me rising from the table. Rounding over to Zalenyk's side I slide on his lap. His short tentacles coast over my face, playing with my hair. Shivering into his touch my fingers explore his face, his groan vibrating me and causing more wetness to slip out of me.

"You know I've never been with anyone before. What will it be like for us?"

"I do not know, I've never been with a human."

"Really?"

"It will be our first time together in a sense."

A small smile curves my lips. "I like that."

We stay silent for a moment, exploring each other. My hands stroke over his face, his chest, tangling in his mass of tentacles. That oily substance I felt yesterday coats my fingers, making them slick. His tentacles have grown and expanded, coasting over my chest, rubbing my hard nipples softly eliciting a moan from my mouth.

Suddenly, I feel it. That hardness beneath my ass pressing against me impatiently. I give a little wiggle and Zalenyk grits his teeth, his tentacles coasting over me faster.

"Zalenyk?"

"Yes, sweet one," he says, his own voice deeper with arousal.

"I want to please you like you pleased me yesterday. You know, with my mouth." My Kraken stops breathing, stops moving, and still I press on. "Will you show me how?"

He doesn't answer, but he moves quickly. Wrapping me up in his arms he takes me from the dining room, so quickly the world is a blur around me. We go deep into the bowels of the castle, and with a wave of his tentacles, the deep water subsides and I find myself in a bedroom.

Not unlike the one I stayed in upstairs but this one seems to find itself submerged quite often. The walls and bedding are wet. The once fine carpet is pulling away and seaweed litters the floor.

Zalenyk's bedroom will definitely need some renovating if we are to be sharing it regularly. That is a problem for another time. Right now I need to be naked, I need him to be naked.

Gently, he lays me on the bed, the waterlogged sheets soaking into my gown. Looming above me I watch with glee as he sheds his more human form and twists into that mass of tentacles and power. The blue muscles slip up along my body, the bed, touching me everywhere.

"Zalenyk." I moan as one tentacle suctions to my nipple over my gown. "I want you so much. Please, I ache for you."

"Melody," he groans, his mouth swooping down on mine. He is soft and slippery, so strong that he could easily crush me. Zalenyk's touches are gentle and exploratory and his tentacles join my own hands as I rip at my gown. Tearing it off of my body until my breasts are free, then my stomach, until I am totally bare.

I feel his tentacles loop around my calves, and my thighs, holding them open as he slips between my legs. My pussy is so wet and sensitive I can't help myself and rub it along him. My own wetness mixed with his own secretions, making my body so sensitive and slick it's a wonder some part of him hasn't already slipped inside of me.

My hands come up to tangle in his tentacles. His tongue dances with mine, licking into my mouth and drinking my moans. I grip the shorter ones around his face until I start moving lower, into the mass of them below. Pulling and tugging to bring him closer to me. My nipples are so hard they are painful and when one of his tentacles suctions onto the tight buds I scream, gripping another tentacle tightly in my hand.

Zalenyk jerks and I feel a rush of more secretion on my hand. Only this one is thicker, stickier, not the clear oily substance as the rest of him.

My eyes fly open and I look into his face, those red eyes clouded with lust.

"You want to please me, little human?"

"Yes."

"That's my cock in your hand. Keep touching it and I'll reward you with my seed."

My smile is so wide it hurts my mouth and I tug at his cock over and over again. It is massive and decorated with smooth ridges and bumps. Looking down I can see it is a darker blue than the rest of him, especially the bulbous head. A trail of white come, coats my hand but I keep moving my fist up and down on him.

His tentacles continue coursing along my body. One sneaks up to wrap around my neck loosely, holding me in place.

"Open your mouth, Melody." I do so immediately. "I love your fire, how strong you are, but make no mistake. In this bed, you are mine. My little human toy whose only purpose is to please me. I will use all of your holes when I see fit and you will beg me for it."

I start to shake my head, the way he's talking, ignites something inside of me. The want to fight him, to scratch, to claw, to make him work to pleasure me.

"I don't beg, Kraken," I say, giving his cock an extra firm tug. He is at my mercy, I am the one with the power here.

His mouth curves into a cruel smile. "Oh my sweet one, that couldn't be farther from the truth. Would you like me to prove it to you?"

"Do your worst." Zalenyk pauses for a second, his eyes growing serious.

"If anything we do—if anything I do—that is too much for you, Melody, tell me to stop. I want complete control of you, but that doesn't mean I just get to have it. Tell me to stop and I stop, understand."

"I want to give you complete control." My Kraken chuckles softly.

"Then tell me you understand what I just said."

"I understand. I say stop you stop." I look him in the eyes while I say the words and part of me melts like sugar in water. Now I just have to see what he does with this new dynamic established between us. A wicked smile curves his lips.

Without warning my hands are ripped away from him. Tentacles wrap around my wrists, pinning them above my head, my chest rising slightly from the bed. The limb wrapped around my throat tightens slightly, as another one snakes along my chest, over my chin, and into my mouth. The tentacles suction onto my tongue and I moan around it, at this new invasion.

It slips in deeper, down my throat until it bumps along the back. My eyes water, and saliva pools in my mouth and along my chin but it keeps going, deep and then retreating, over and over again.

"Take it, my pretty little slut, get it nice and wet so when I put it in your asshole it slides in nicely."

I start to thrash in his grip. My *ass*? Surely not.

When it finally subsides from my mouth, I cough and sputter. His eyes gleam with a wickedness I have not seen before.

"I can do whatever I want to you. Restrain you, choke you, and you know that you'll still walk away from this being my treasure. Don't you?"

Shaking my head again his grip on my throat tightens.

"Don't lie to me."

"Yes, yes I'm still your treasure."

"That's right," he purrs, feeling more tentacles loop around my legs they are hoisted into the air and pushed back against my chest. I'm completely exposed to his eyes, my glistening pussy swollen and begging for his attention. "But right now you're my human whore and I have to remind you who owns you."

That is all the warning I get before his tongue reaches out and licks me from pussy to asshole. It delves between the cheeks of my ass and prods the tight ring of muscles. Dipping in slightly and then retreating.

"Zalenyk, not there!" I scream, the sensation is foreign but not altogether unpleasant. I like what he is doing, I realize. His harsh words and degradation should be a turn-off to me, as they would be from any man, but Zalenyk is right. Here I can find him and let him own me. It is the one place I feel safe being overpowered. He is the one person who can overpower me and yet when this is over will treat me like I am his most prized treasure.

That knowledge lets me sink into this, into him, and lose myself to this coupling.

"Here." His tongue presses in deeper, his saliva coating my hole. "There." A tentacle comes up to gently dip into my pussy. His oily substance makes me even wetter. I am so full and so completely owned it is glorious.

"Wherever I want, whenever I want."

"No." I could tell him to stop if I really wanted to and I know he would, but stopping him is the last thing I want to do.

"Yes. Here you submit to me."

"Make me."

Zalenyk chuckles darkly and then it begins. His tongue leaves my ass only to be replaced by the tentacle that was in my mouth. It circles me there, once, then twice until it slips in gently. The burn makes my back arch.

His tongue is at my pussy, lapping up my entrance before moving up to suck on my clit.

"Such a pretty pussy, Melody. You're lucky no man ever had you. If he had, if he dared to see this pussy, my pussy, I'd have to kill him. Drown him in the sea and make him watch as I fucked you."

I cry out, my hands straining to grab onto anything, but I am powerless. At the mercy of my Kraken, all I can do is ride out this experience and hope I come out the other side in one piece.

His tongue parts me, tasting me as my moisture leaks out of me. The tentacles wrapped around my legs push them back even further until my hips raise off the bed. I am a meal to this creature and he is going to feast on me. Over and over again he licks me, dipping inside and then giving the same treatment to my clit.

The tentacle at my ass spears in deeper and I cry out.

Another one sneaks up to sink gently into my pussy. They work me in tandem, in shallow thrusts as Zalenyk sucks on my clit. My muscles tighten, my pussy clenching down on.

"My little slut has the tightest cunt known to man. Are you close? Do you want me to make you come?"

"Yes!" I'm desperate too, my eyes water and I pull against his hold on my arms. My thighs begin to shake, and I move my hips in time with his tentacles, needing that extra bit of friction to push me over the edge.

"Hmmm," Zalenyk hums in his throat. "I don't think my little fucktoy has earned it yet. After all, she hasn't made me come as a good girl should."

Everything stops.

His tentacles leave me, and so does his mouth. My muscles quiver and I scream, trying desperately to get him back, to throw myself over the edge. Tears burn in my eyes from disappointment from denial.

"What the fuck? Make me come, Kraken!" I scream, foul language slipping from me again.

Zalenyk only laughs before using his tentacles to flip me. I'm suspended in the air while he slips up into the bed. He brings me back down so my face is on top of his great mass of tentacles and my ass is in his face. A sharp sting hits my backside and I realized he's smacked my ass with his tentacle. I feel the heat from it bloom ling on my skin.

"Naughty girl, you don't speak to your master like that."

"My master is supposed to make me come!" I cry. My lip juts out and I feel sweat beading at my brow. I'm not above throwing a temper tantrum right now. The denial of my orgasm burns so hotly inside me. I try to rock back onto his face but he stops me.

"I'll make you come, my sweet. After you behave like a good girl and make me come down your pretty little throat."

With that new goal in mind, my arms are free, and fling myself down into his massive body. It's not hard to find his cock, it stands out from the rest of his tentacles. Thicker than the rest of his tentacles and devoid of all suckers. It's darker in color and decorated with ridges and bumps along the shaft. I've never done anything like this before but I let instinct take over.

Giving him a tentative lick I taste his salty sweetness and decide I could dine on this. I lick him again before taking the head into my mouth. Sucking lightly I use my hand to circle his shaft, stroking at the same time. He's so large I doubt I'll get him all the way down my throat but I am determined to try.

"So good, my treasure. So perfect, I knew you were born to suck my cock."

I moan around his length, my own wetness leaking out of me. As if he can't help himself I feel his tongue sneak up to lick between my slit. Groaning at my taste and renewed by that bit of pleasure I work his cock harder. My head bobs as I cram him down my throat further.

My lips stretch wide and I feel him bump against the back of my throat. My eyes burn but I keep going, briefly realizing he was testing me earlier like this with his tentacle. Getting me prepared for this exact moment. I fight past the burn and feel him slip down my throat, more salty goodness spurts into my mouth.

Swallowing down eagerly, he groans and that's when I feel him at my entrances. A tentacle probes my pussy and my ass, his tongue tickling my clit. Not with the vigor he did before but enough to know that my reward is coming soon.

I double my efforts, licking and sucking, running my tongue along each bump and ridge. How will this feel inside of me? I can't wait to find out.

"Do you want me to fill your holes, Melody?"

"Yes," I gasp, finally releasing his length with a pop.

"Then ask me." I grit my teeth, and my old vow that I don't beg rings in my ears but I'm done pretending that's not true. I'll beg if he lets me come.

"Please, Zalenyk, please use my holes. Make me come, master, please."

Zalenyk chuckles and then his mouth is on me. Glancing over my shoulder, I watch his massive blue tentacles push into me, in and out. Moving in fluid motions together. I hear him sucking on my clit, the wet and sloppy sounds my pussy is making. The sight before me is so erotically beautiful, I fall back on his cock and work him with the same intensity.

My thighs shake once more. This orgasm feels more intense as if being denied the first time has caused my body to rage. I might snap in half once he finally lets me come but I won't stop sucking on his cock. It hardens in my mouth and his tentacles seem to pulse around me.

"Close, Melody?"

Nodding, I don't dare release him from my mouth.

"Me too. Swallow it all down, sweet one." That's the only warning I get before a roar so loud it shakes the room around me. Then I'm drowning in his seed. So much sprays from his cock and shoots down my throat. I try and swallow all of it down but I can't quite manage it. It leaks from every tentacle, coating me in that sticky substance.

It covers my face and chest, some is in my hair, and of course in my stomach. There's so much of it I can only moan and writhe as it coats me completely.

Then my own orgasm hits me.

Sneaking up on me like an eel in the water, I go up in flames. My muscles seize, my body shakes and I scream.

Scream for Zalenyk, scream for mercy, scream for anything. The warm press of his tongue is at my entrance as he drinks down my come.

I lay there on him, shaking with little aftershocks, sticky from his seed, and panting.

My throat and eyes burn, my muscles are aching, and there are red sucker marks all over my body. Yet, I have never, ever been happier.

Tentacles flip me and suddenly I am staring at Zalenyk's face. He wipes some of his seed from my cheek with a gentle touch. There is a soft rushing sound before warm water glides through the air washing away his seed from my body and hair and off him as well. There is a wariness to him.

"Are you alright, my treasure? I didn't hurt you did I?"

I shake my head no and bury it into his warmth.

"I need the words, Melody." His tone is firm and almost pleading.

"Zalenyk," I murmur into his chest. "I loved it. Every second of it. You gave me something I never knew I needed."

"What's that?" He pulls me closer to him.

"An outlet. To be wild and free; to be able to fight you and you still want me after."

"I more than want you, Melody." Kissing the top of my head, I want to tell him that I more than want him too. "I promised to give you everything that you need and I will not fail you on that."

"There is one thing I need though." My fingers tangle in his tentacles, wrapping a few of them around my fist.

"What is that, my sweet?"

I smile, running my tongue along the side of his face. Salty and sweet, maybe I should call him sweet one as well.

"I need you to come inside me this time."

6

MELODY

Zalenyk freezes, his tentacles pausing they're playing along my hair.

Surely this can't be a surprise to him. Sucking him off was nice, but it just made me want to feel him inside me even more. Slinging my leg over him, I straddle his massive form. Red splotches decorate my chest where his tentacles sucked on me.

"Don't you want to give me that?" I pout. "Haven't I been good enough to earn more of your come?"

His tentacles come up to dig into my backside, wrap around my hips and hold me in place to stop my wiggling.

"You have been good," he says. "Do you want me inside that little pussy? My tentacle wasn't enough, was it? You need to be stuffed with my cock, greedy slut."

"Yes." Nodding my head vigorously. "I want your cock so bad, please. I've saved myself for you."

"When I come inside you, Melody, you know what could happen?" he asks.

"Yes," I answer, trying in vain to move my hips.

"You'd want that? Me to breed you?"

"Isn't that why you stole me? Deep, deep down that was always your plan?" I ask, even if we are playing this game between us I want to hear his answer. It will determine where I take it from here.

"Did I take you so I could fill you with my come, over and over again?" He curls a lock of hair around his tentacle. "Yes, I suppose I did. The thought did occur to me that I could get you pregnant, despite me telling you that I wanted my kind to end with me."

"Do you still want that?"

"I want you," he says, firmly. "If you want us to have a child, I will love it just as I love you." My eyes water at his confession. "If you do not, I will procure you herbs that will stop your womb from quickening. Your choice, sweet one, always yours."

I lean down and press my mouth to his.

"I love you too," I say, it feels too soon but I'm about to fuck a Kraken. I think I can let my human reflex to play aloof fade. It is the truth, it is how I really feel. No mask, no guard. I will only be my true self in front of Zalenyk. "I'll take the herbs, there are so many things I want to see. To experience with you."

"I'll show you everything, Melody. My treasure, my love." Zalenyk kisses me again, his tongue slipping in my mouth, his body raising beneath me. I pull back slightly, running a hand down over my pale, flat stomach.

"One day, though, I want us to have a child. I want us to have a family."

"Anything you want, Melody."

"I knew you'd say that," I laugh. "Now fuck me until I can't walk."

I'm rolled onto my back, my arms and legs wrapped up in his tentacles. Splayed open wide like an offering. One limb sneaks around and slithers into my opening. My wetness mixed with Zalenyk's own has the tentacle easily pushing inside of me. A second one is added but even that I realize pales in comparison to Zalenyk's actual size.

The sensation still makes me moan, feeling so full I could burst. His tongue licks over my breast, circling each pale pink nipple until it is a stiff peak. My mouth is empty for a moment and as if he realizes that, my Kraken pushes one of his tentacles inside. I suck on it like I did his cock and he growls, as it tickles the back of my throat.

"Would you like to be filled now?" Zalenyk asks. I nod my head vigorously. "The words, Melody. Don't make me remind you again."

"Yes, Zalenyk, my love, my master, fill me. I'm so empty without you."

He groans and my legs are pushed apart even wider. Something hard rubs along my entrance. It presses firmly against my clit and I squirm before I feel it dip inside of me. The head of his cock has barely breached me and already I feel stretched beyond belief.

"Zalenyk—"

"Shh, you can take it. I own this pretty pussy and it will welcome me." He leans down and plants a kiss on my lips. "I just need to give it a bit of a push."

I can tell he tries to be gentle, but between his size and my small frame, there's no way to avoid the uncomfortable pressure. Realizing with some mild horror that he isn't even halfway inside of me and I already feel like I'm about ready to burst. He stills, letting some of his own natural lubricant help the situation. It does the trick and he slides a few more inches in. My breath catches. We do this same motion over and over again until he's fully seated inside me.

There was a slight tear and a small pinch that brought a

rush of tears to my eyes. Zalenyk wipes them away with a tentacle. He remains still while my body adjusts, giving me a few shallow thrusts.

"You're doing so well, sweet one. You take me so well in this little cunt of yours."

Sliding himself back so that only the head of his cock remains in me, he thrusts forward and I realize the pain is gone. Our combined moisture has done the trick. All I want now is more.

A tentacle snakes out and massages my clit, suctioning onto it. I feel so incredibly full, but I need him to start moving. Really moving. I start rocking my hips in order to create some more delicious friction. Those ridges and bumps I tasted earlier along his cock are pure heaven inside of me.

Helping to tickle a spot deep inside of me that has my vision blurring.

"Greedy for my cock, aren't you?"

"Yes!" I cry and he rewards me with a shallow thrust.

"You came to me a virgin but you'll become my whore in no time. Look at you, working yourself on my cock, pathetically trying to fuck yourself on me."

"I need more, Zalenyk, please."

He pulls back out of me and then thrusts forward. My breast bounce in time with his fucking and I throw my head back absorbing each blow. Zalenyk goes slow, stoking the fire inside of me. Despite his harsh words, he's being gentle with me.

Too gentle.

"I thought you were going to fuck me until I couldn't walk?" I ask in a put-out tone.

"Is that not what I'm doing?" He grits out, one tentacle coming to wrap around my throat.

"Fuck me harder, faster!" I demand, trying to move my hips to capture more of him.

He stops moving completely, his red eyes narrowing.

"You want it rough, little slut?"

"Only if you think you can do it. At this point, it seems like me, the virgin, is the one fucking you." Zalenyk laughs darkly, withdrawing from me completely. I whine at the loss of sensation. I want him back, I crave it.

His tentacles flip me over onto my front, before roughly lifting my ass high. A few limbs wrap around my arms and keep them tied behind my back. Another set slides my feet apart so I am fully exposed and unable to close them.

"You don't know what you've asked for." I watch from below as his tentacle snaps out and slaps my ass. The heat from the sting makes my pussy grow even wetter. "You're the Kraken's little come slut, aren't you? I was trying to treat you nicely for your first time, but you don't want that do you? You want me to use all of your little holes?"

"Yes!" I cry. "Use me, however, you want."

I feel him slip up behind me and line his cock up with my pussy.

"I plan to."

Zalenyk slams into me so hard that I almost tumble forward. If not for the strong grip his tentacles have on my arms and legs I would've fallen. He pounds into me so hard, over and over again. The sound of our body slapping together fills the room. The wet slide of his cock in and out of me. It is so obscenely beautiful.

I moan into the mattress, unable to do anything but accept each one of his thrusts. My clit is being sucked on by one of his tentacles, and another one prods my ass, before slipping inside. Being filled so crudely in this way turns a key in me. I love his treatment, I love everything about this.

"Such a tight cunt," he grunts, "you'll be this tight every time I fuck you? Of course, you will, you want to please me."

"Yes, yes," I pant. The sensation is too much. My hair sticks to the sweat on my brow. From my bound position, my arms are beginning to ache but I don't tell him to stop. I want it to keep going, to see what cliff this leads me to so I can be thrown off of it.

A tentacle winds around my hair and my head is snapped up. My back arches to accommodate this new position and I am vaguely aware I'm being lifted from the bed. Another pair of tentacles come up to knead and suction my breasts. My moans are louder and wilder. A warmth spreads low in my stomach. It is heightened when I watch my skin become shiny with Zalenyk's own fluid, coating me and making me tingle.

The limbs holding me aloft suddenly move and I'm being thrust back on Zalenyk as he thrust forward. These rough thrusts make my eyes start to close. That beautifully ridged cock of his tickles that hidden spot and my muscles tighten. My neck strains as it is snatched back even further. The muscles of my pussy clench down around him and I hear Zalenyk growl.

"Does my human whore want to come?" I shake my head as best I can in this position. "Beg me."

"I can't—it's—it's too much!" He freezes, and I scream at the loss of movement. Suddenly I am ripped off of his cock and I feel it press against my ass.

"Beg me, Melody or my cock goes in here and I'll make you beg me to come with it stuffed in your ass."

"No please, I'll beg, I'll beg." Still, he doesn't move away from my back entrance.

"I'm waiting."

"Please, Zalenyk, please fuck my pussy. Please come

inside of me, I want you to. Reward me with your seed, I need to feel it drip out of me." My Kraken sinks back inside my pussy and begins his punishing pace again. My thighs tremble my chest heaves. I am close, so close.

"Tell me that you love that I took you. Tell me that you'll always be mine."

"I love that you took me! You saved me, Zalenyk. I'm yours, I'll always be yours."

That snaps something inside him and he doubles his efforts. Each stab of his cock inside me unlocks pure euphoria. My muscles strain and then I am thrown off of that cliff. My orgasm is ripped from me, a scream ringing in my ears as my pussy clamps down on him. This climax is painful, so overwhelming that tears leak from my eyes.

So many things clash inside me at once, but through them, the only thing I feel is how right this is. How much I completely and totally belong to my Kraken.

Just as I start to come down, Zalenyk tightens his tentacle around my throat and lets out a roar. I feel the come explode out of him and into me. Burning hot, it seeps from his cock and his tentacles until I am once again coated in his spend. He fucks it into me and that sets off another orgasm.

Not so world-shattering as the first one but definitely enough to have my toes curling.

Sticky and panting, Zalenyk releases me from his hold and slowly pulls out of me. I feel the rush of his come slide down my thighs and onto the mattress below. Smiling, I slump forward onto the mattress, unable to move.

My body is still quivering with little aftershocks as Zalenyk rolls me onto my back. Looking down at me with wonder and love in his eyes. I hope mine are reflecting the same thing because that is how I feel at this moment.

"You did so good, Melody. You are so perfect." I blush

and smile softly. He comes around to lay at my side and I nuzzle into him. I know my blush is even deeper when I spy the red mark on the bed.

Just like before, another rush of warm water comes and cleans us both off.

"As soon as I can move, I want to do that again," I say, yawning into his chest. He cocoons me in his massive, meaty limbs.

"Whatever you want, Melody, you know that."

I do, I think as I begin to nod off. Warm and satisfied with my Kraken's come leaking out of me I realize that even if I did have the choice to leave here I wouldn't. I want to stay just like this forever.

7

MELODY

It's dark in Zalenyk's room when I finally open my eyes.

My Kraken is still asleep beside me, massive body rising and following with each great breath. I could've only been asleep for a few hours. His tentacles are still curled around me, one is even stuck to my cheek.

There was a reason I woke up? I swallow and then I am reminded. Gently disentangling myself from his hold, I grab a discarded blanket, damp and cold, and cover myself. Going in search of a glass of water, I pad down the sodden hallway.

This area of the palace will definitely need some touch-ups.

Making this palace my home warms something inside of me. I was never allowed to decorate at my father's home and while I'm sure gold-crusted light fixtures aren't readily available in this part of the country I can still make it my own.

Even if I wanted gold fixures I know Zalenyk would find a way to get them for me.

As I make my way down the hall, I realize more of his

come leaks out of me and I am a bit tender between my legs. He was so deliciously rough. Once I quench my thirst perhaps I will wake him with my mouth on his cock.

Then we can fuck again. That sounds good to me.

There is a light up ahead and that is what I am following. I'll need a proper tour of this place because this area is completely unfamiliar to me.

As I get closer to the light I can hear raised voices. Moving on quiet feet I duck into what I assume is the kitchen. Finding my discarded glass of wine from dinner, I take a sip. There are a few shouts and loud bangs from the other side of the door.

I should go and wake Zalenyk, perhaps someone is in trouble.

The doors swing open and I can't even comprehend what I am seeing. It is the human captain, unbound and staring right at me as if he also can't believe his eyes. My wine glass slips from my hand and shatters at my feet.

We stare at each other for a beat. I should scream, do something, anything, but fear has frozen me to the spot. He is holding something in his hands that I can't make out in the dim light.

His mouth curves into a smile, exposing his yellowed teeth. "This is perfect."

That's the last thing I hear before he strikes out, hitting me in the side of the head with whatever he was holding. The world around me goes dark as I crumple to the floor

Zalenyk

The lack of Melody's warmth is what wakes me.

Her small breasts are no longer being pressed into my side and that will not do. The area where she was nestled next to me is still warm, so wherever she went she could not have left that long ago. If she needed something she should've woken me up, I would've gladly gotten it for her.

She is mine. All mine, she admitted as much and I will treasure that fact for the rest of eternity. I should be showing her right now how much I love her, to prove to her that she is not wrong for loving me back.

Slipping from the bed I go in search of my sweet little human. What should I do first? Feast on her pink cunt? Lick her little asshole until she shakes? Maybe I'll fuck her with my tentacles until she begs for my cock?

The possibilities with Melody seem endless.

I follow her scent, one that has now mingled with mine, to the kitchen. The honeyed smell of it is so rich, I could come just from inhaling it deeply. Bursting through the kitchen doors I expect to find her there, waiting for me with a smile, naked.

However, she is not.

With some growing alarm, I can also smell another scent in here. Male. Human. I notice the shattered glass in the corner and a small pool of blood. My heart begins to race.

"Melody?" I call. "Melody!"

I barrel into the front room and my servants are scrambling. They all stop in their tracks and turn to look at me.

"Where is she? What has happened?" None of them speak and my anger and confusion only grow.

"Speak," I command, snatching one of the servants and dragging him in front of me.

"The hu—humans escaped, Your Majesty. Your human bride went with them. We saw her climb onto their ship and sail away."

Melody...is gone? She left me?

"Why was I not informed of this?" I growl, gripping him tighter.

"The patrol last night was all killed. A few of us ran after them down the beach to try and stop them and that's when we saw her board and begin to sail off. We were too late to stop them."

My heart sinks. Perhaps I was wrong, perhaps she only said those things to placate me. Has she been plotting with them all along? Knowing they would be her best option to hatch an escape plan. Did she only agree to fuck me so I would be tired enough for her to escape?

Even as I think about it, I know that isn't right.

Melody is brave and strong and she would never have given herself to me if she did not wish to. My gut tells me they took her and if that is the case then they are already dead. She is mine, she belongs to me and I will do whatever it takes to get her back.

"Which direction did they sail?" I ask, my voice deeper. The magic I've contained for so long is released, unfurling from inside me. My servant gulps as I drop him, rising up and expanding to fill the entire front room.

"E—east, Your Majesty."

I haven't been forced into this legendary size in decades, but these humans who dared steal my treasure will face the full force of my wrath. I slither out of the palace into the waiting cold water. Smelling Melody in the air I hold onto that sent, tracking it as any predator would.

I will get back my treasure and those who dared to take her will be led to their watery deaths.

8

MELODY

My head is throbbing and I am freezing cold.

How did everything go from perfect to horrible in the span of a few minutes? I shiver and try and wrap the blanket tighter around myself. The captain is close by, directing the members of his crew and casting me lecherous looks. I shiver again and this time, not from the cold.

"You're lucky I found you when I did," he sneers, coming to loom over me. He smells of sweat and sour ale. "You should be grateful I'm saving you from that creature. And with you on board, he'll think twice about attacking our ship."

He reaches out and takes a lock of my hair between his fingers and I jerk away.

"This hair will fetch a high price when we get to port. You all together will. That'll serve that bastard Kraken right for stealing our cargo. We'll sell his treasure to the highest bidder."

"The only bastard here is you!" I seeth. "He will come for me and when he does you will all be dead."

The captain laughs, grabbing a fist full of my hair so I have to look up at him. The pressure on my scalp makes my eyes water.

"I doubt he's even realized your gone, by the time he does we will be far away from here." He releases me and stomps away. "Now be quiet or I'll have to find some way to keep you silent. You really wouldn't enjoy that."

The sky is still dark as we cut through the open sea. I try and make myself small, tucking into the corner of the deck. The skies open up and rain descends down upon us. I'm soaking and so cold, and my breath curls in a white cloud in front of me. Zalenyk, where is he?

Surely he has noticed my absence by now.

The only reason I boarded this ship is by the time I came too I was already being hauled onto the deck. A few of the crew members tried grabbing at my covering and I yanked it free of their grips. If I had the chance to run I would've at least tried.

I can only send a prayer up that Zalenyk notices and he gets to me in time before we make it to port.

"Brace yourselves!" yells the captain.

The water has gotten choppy. Large waves are illuminated by flashes of lightning. The air is salty. Cold, dark water splashes over the sides of the deck and soaks me. Between the rain and the water, I may freeze to death before I make it to our destination.

Perhaps if I drown, my soul will be sent back to Zalenyk.

I shake myself from that dark thought. He has to be coming for me, I know he is. Our ship continues in the rough water. Dipping and bobbing, a few of the crew are sick over the side of the boat. There is an ominous creak and crack. A flash of lightning illuminates something in the distance.

"What is that!" someone cries, but I see it all the same. I see him.

Zalenyk is here, just like I knew he would be. His massive frame rises out of the water. His tentacles were far-reaching, his head as large and as wide as four ship lengths. The power radiating off of him makes me grow wet.

I love him and he's here to rescue me.

This form is the one legends were born from. He is formidable and scary, a god of the sea. A god that I am raising on shaking legs and walking towards the front of the boat to go and see. Salty water doses me again and those massive red eyes track my every movement.

The crew scatters behind me, cowering in fear.

"Zalenyk," I cry, waving my arm. "You saved me again. You always save me."

"I'd do anything for you, Melody." I laugh and tears stream down my cheeks.

I need to be back in his embrace, to feel his warm body against mine. To burrow so far inside of him that there is no separating us. Dropping the blanket, I step over the railing at the front of the ship and plunge into the dark water below.

It's so quiet underneath the surface I almost forget what is waging above. Then I feel it, a meaty tentacle slipping between my legs and along my front. It is so wide I can barely get my arms and legs around it but I hold on for dear life as it lifts me out of the water.

Zalenyk brings me in front of his face, so large and so worried. I must look like a doll to him at this size. He pulls me in closer until I am flush against his cheek. I run my hand along it and nuzzle into the tentacle holding me.

"Are you alright, my love?" he asks, his voice so deep it sends ripples into the ocean below us.

"I am now. I knew you'd save me."

"So you did not wish to leave with them?" he asks carefully, and my hand freezes. I squeeze his tentacle and he circles me around to the front of his face.

"Zalenyk, I told you I never want to leave you. I'm yours forever, just as you are mine."

"My Melody, my treasure," he murmurs reverently. "They tried to take you from me and they failed. Watch what happens to anyone who dares to try and steal you."

With a powerful rush of water, I can see Zalenyk lift one meaty tentacle from the water and smash it down onto their boat. I hear the wood splinter and the crew scream for mercy. I watch as Zalenyk holds them all below the surface, locked in a tight grip of his tentacles until they drown.

The wicked shiver that passes through me at the sight does not escape his notice.

"Did that make your little pussy wet, Melody? To see me take all their lives as payment for trying to take you from me."

"Whenever I'm around you my pussy is always wet."

"Hmmm," he groans, "let me see just how wet you are."

Then I am being dangled in front of him. His massive pale blue tongue slips from his mouth and runs up along my body. My arms are held tightly in his tentacles and his tongue keeps me seated. It's easy four times my size and licks me from between my ass to my nipples.

"At this size, you really are my little fucktoy."

His tongue is so warm and wet and before long my toes are curling. Zalenyk is everywhere, as soaked with him as I am with the rain. He owns me but I own him too and that's why he is the only one who will ever get me this way.

"I love you," I babble, my orgasm quickly approaching.

"I love you, Melody."

My body seizes and my Kraken is there, licking up my come and tucking me against him. Curling into his warmth I do not stir again until the morning sun has risen.

EPILOGUE

ZALENYK - ONE YEAR LATER

Life in the Drowned Palace is absolutely perfect.

Especially because Melody is there. Every day with her is more perfect than the last. In the past year, I can honestly say that my life has never had more meaning, being filled with so much joy and love that I can hardly believe my luck. Melody is my treasure and each day with her is a gift.

But a gift is what I have left the warmth of her thighs to go and find.

While I call her my bride I have yet to make her my wife. It is a small thing, a human thing, but I want Melody tied to me in as many ways as I can get her. That is why I have ventured so far from the sea and into *The Woods.* Why I stand before the door of the demon who lives in them and knock once.

Behind it, I can hear the faint sound of a woman's cries. I think she could be in pain but then it is followed by a moan and I realize what keeps this beast from answering my summons. Even if I understand the feeling. If it was a choice between Melody and talking to this beast, I wouldn't answer my door either.

Still, I knock again.

There is a small giggle, followed by thunderous footsteps. The old door is nearly torn from the hinges and the demon of *The Woods* stands before me naked. Eyes of pure fire glower at me.

"What do you want, Kraken?" He grits out, I've clearly caught him at a bad time so better to make this quick.

"The pearls that a fisherman traded with you to steal my fish, do you still have them?" The demon smirks and reaches to the side of the door. Chuckling, the demon squeezes the small bag of pearls in his clawed hand and shakes his head.

"An unwise bargain for that fisherman I take it."

I am poised to agree but then I remember what I got out of it. Melody. Without his theft, I would've never met her.

"On the contrary, this turned out quite fruitful for me."

"My love?" calls a delicate female voice from deep inside the demon's cottage. He practically shoves the pearls in my hands, bracing his hand on the door frame.

"Be gone, Kraken, I have more important matters to attend to."

"You do not want the rubies I brought? Stole them from a king's merchant ship." I tap the pouch at my side. "My Melody doesn't much care for them, but I thought you might have some use for them."

"A human?" asks the demon, pausing in shutting the door, his nostrils flaring as he registers the other scent on me. From the scent inside the house, I can tell he has one himself.

"I see you've found yourself besotted by one as well." The demon smiles slightly and nods.

"My Irys doesn't have much care for them either. The

Dragon's Lair isn't too far from here, if you really want to part with them he'll surely take them off your hands."

"He's stirring again? It's been decades since I last heard he was awake."

"He was always the most miserable amongst us," the demon replied. Another call from deep within the house stops me from asking any more questions. "Be gone."

The door slams with a final thud.

I'm still standing on the stoop when I hear the moaning pick back up again. It reminds me of Melody and how I need to get back to her as soon as possible. This trip to the Dragon's Lair will be fast and then I will be back inside her again.

Cutting through *The Woods* it is not long before I find myself at the mouth of a giant cave. Even with the bright sun beating down on me, only about five feet into the mouth of the cave are visible. I've never been inside of it, no humans have and have lived to tell the tale.

My natural aversion to fire has never made me want to stay in this place for very long, nor in the presence of the dragon himself. Asgorath is right, he was always the most miserable among us.

Though a curse will do that to you, I suppose.

Setting the bag down I leave it just inside the cave's mouth. Within a second two fiery eyes emerge from the darkness. The sun illuminates shiny scales and razor-sharp black claws that snatch the bag away from the opening and deep into the darkness.

"Silly creature," I say, not knowing or caring if he can even keep me. "I hope one day you find that there is something more precious than jewels and gold out there."

Mine is currently waiting for me in our bed.

I move quickly back out of *The Woods*. The river is

rushing nearby and I transform as I close in on it. Changing from my humanoid form to my real one and using the power of my tentacles to swim me home as quickly as possible. I keep the bag of pearls tucked in my tentacles. The water moves past me in a flurry of bubbles. I barely spare a passing glance at the creatures I swim by.

My mind is focused on my treasure.

It takes me too long to make it back to the palace. Too long until I am inside my bedroom and come face to face with Melody. She's still asleep, her red hair fanned out all around her. Our lovemaking last night and into this morning was particularly vigorous so I know she's wiped out.

One long, pale leg lays above the sheets and I cannot resist running a tentacle along it. Her blue eyes blink open and she smiles, stretching her arms out and sitting up. The white sheet slips down her body until her breasts are free, covered only by the tresses of her hair.

I slide onto the bed and wrap her in my tentacles. Kissing my lips, she burrows into my side.

"You smell like the ocean. Where have you been?" My tongue suddenly feels too big for my mouth and I swallow loudly. She furrows her red brows. "What?"

"I went to retrieve something." A tentacle I had tucked tightly to my chest, unwinds from me holding out the small bag of pearls. Melody gasps and grabs it from me. Her delicate hands are shaking as she holds it, as she opens it, and sifts through the contents.

"Zalenyk," she gasps, "how on earth did you find these?"

"The demon and I have known each other for ages. I persuade him to let me have them."

Her hands dig through the bag and pull out a small stand necklace of pearls.

"She always wore this." Her voice is hoarse with unshed tears. Next, she pulls out a small ring with a pearl at the center. The rest of the bag is just filled with loose pearls. Black, white, and silver.

Melody cradles the ring to her chest. "This was her favorite ring, the one she wanted my husband to give to me when he proposed." Her laugh is watery. "Thank you, Zalenyk, there are no words to describe what this means to me. What you mean to me, my love."

She smiles up at me and I gently take the ring from her, holding it out to her.

"Melody, I love you. I'll love you forever. I want to make you my wife, my partner, and when the time comes, the mother of my children." She nods and with the help of my tentacles, I slide the ring onto her finger, a perfect fit. "There is no service that needs to be performed. I am king here and I declare us wed."

"There you go again, making your own rules." She flings herself at me, peppering my face with kisses. "Husband." We both moan over the title.

Then our mouths are connected and everything inside of me is right once more. I can feel her pussy dripping onto me. My tentacle comes up to circle her entrance before slipping inside. Nice and deep until she moans into my mouth. I swallow the sound.

"Which hole do you want me in first, wife?" Her smile is deviant and daring and so full of love.

"All of them."

The End

ACKNOWLEDGMENTS

Hello! Thank you so much for reading A Kiss From a Kraken. I hoped you loved Melody and Zalenyk's love story as much as I did! A dragon novella is coming later this year so stay tuned for that! If you want to read any of my other works they are linked ahead.

Xoxo Charlotte

ABOUT THE AUTHOR

Charlotte Swan is twenty-four year old, living in Chicago. When she is not dreaming about being whisked away to a world filled with magic and sexy monsters, she is busy being a freelance social media marketer and full-time smut lover. To read her debut novel *Taken by the Dark Elf King*, hear about her upcoming projects, or to connect with her on social media please find her on her website or by scanning the code below.

www.authorcharlotteswan.com

ALSO BY CHARLOTTE SWAN

Kiss From a Monster Series

A Kiss From a Demon (Kiss From a Monster Series Book 1)

Irys Evergrove only wanted one thing: to avoid marriage to the lecherous duke that has desired her long before she came of age. Those in her village speak of a demon that lives in *The Woods*, a magical land that very few humans dare to enter. Her desperation sends her into the heart of the forest until she comes face to face with a creature pulled straight from her nightmares.

So why does he excite her in a way no mortal man ever has?

Begging him to save her from her marriage he agrees but refuses the meager amount of coins she offers him. What this demon desires from her is one pleasure-filled night with her in his cottage. This demon unlocks something inside of Irys she has long since buried. When the sun rises in the morning will she truly be able to start her new life with the freedom she bargained for? Or will she realize that the passion she found between her and the demon of *The Woods* is not something so easily found again?

Monstrous Mates Series

Taken by the Dark Elf King (Monstrous Mates Series Book 1)

Princess Elveena has never seen a dark elf in her life.

As princess of the light of elves, their two kinds have been separated since before her birth. When a royal messenger arrives inviting them to a ball hosted by the king of the dark elves, Elvie knows she cannot pass up on this once in a lifetime opportunity.

Even after the warnings from her father, Elvie knows this will be a night she'll never forget.

She expected to end the night with sore feet from the endless hours of dancing...***not to be engaged to the king himself!***

Trapped in this new kingdom, Elvie knows she must make the most of her new situation. With each passing day she learns that King Arkain is not what she thought a dark elf would be like. Sure he is mean and beastly compared to the males she is used to but, Elvie quickly finds that to be the reason he excites her so much.

As the threat of war looms, will this budding passion between Elvie and the king continue to blossom? Or will she lose herself and all that she loves in the process?

Captured by the Orc General (Monstrous Mates Series Book 2)

Royal alchemist Kaethe knows two things:

1 Drinking tea made from steeped riverhearts will cure almost anything.

2 Never, ever trust an orc.

But when a rumor, that she believes pertains to her missing brother, has her leaving the safety and warmth of King Arkain and Queen Elvie's court she finds herself in the heart of the orc's territory. Brokenbone Mountain is rumored to be filled with unspeakable danger. And if you are able to survive the harsh elements, those foul creatures that call the mountain home will enjoy feasting on your bones.

Delightful.

Bazur, General of the Black Claw Clan, has no time for humans. The years have turned him as cold as the mountain he calls home. The last thing he needs turning up in one of his traps is a brightly-colored hair human, who danger seems to be following like a shadow. Bazur should turn her away and let the beasts have an easy dinner. But there is something about her that stops him. That propels him to take her in and to keep her safe.

Even if she seems terrified of him.

When one of his clan-mates falls ill, Kaethe is the only one able to save him. In return, Bazur promises her safe passage through the mountain and he will act as her overseer while she sets about finding her brother.

As the nights on Brokenbone mountain grow longer and colder, both Kaethe and Bazur discover new things about each other. Will the distrust they harbor for each others kind give way to the passion brewing between them? Or will forces beyond their control separate them before they get the chance?

Made in the USA
Columbia, SC
20 March 2025